Romantic Times has raved about Barbara McMahon's **Western Weddings,** and awarded *Wyoming Wedding,* the first in the trilogy, an excellent 4 ½ gold rating:

Wyoming Wedding
"Top-notch storyteller Barbara McMahon brings vivid characters to life that will endear themselves to readers, along with clever and ingenious dialogue."

Angel Bride
"Creates a truly unforgettable story."

Bride on the Ranch
"Outstanding storyteller Barbara McMahon gives us another brilliant tale...a high level of passion, humor and emotion that will leave you begging for more."

Dear Reader,

Bride on the Ranch is the third book in my
Western Weddings series. It is Kyle Carstairs's story.
Combining two of my favorite careers—ranching and
writing—I tried to present the perfect setting for two very
different people to fall in love. My delight in the state of
Wyoming again shows itself in the location of the Carstairs
ranch, not too far from Cheyenne.

I've been on horse drives where we rode for days without
seeing any signs of mankind except for barbed wire
fences, and I've stayed on working ranches. In this book I
tried to capture some of the feelings I've experienced
playing cowboy. Of course, in *Bride on the Ranch* there are
authentic cowboys, open ranges, distant mountains and
cooling breezes. Welcome to the American West!

For this last book about the Carstairs family, I've brought
back Angel and Jake, Rafe and Charity, and the newest
generation of Carstairses.

If you've enjoyed the stories of Rafe, Angelica and Kyle,
do write and let me know. I hope you've had as much fun
sharing their adventures as I've had writing them!

Yours,

Barbara McMahon
P.O. Box 977
Pioneer, CA 95666
U.S.A.

Bride on
the Ranch
Barbara McMahon

Harlequin Books

TORONTO • NEW YORK • LONDON
AMSTERDAM • PARIS • SYDNEY • HAMBURG
STOCKHOLM • ATHENS • TOKYO • MILAN
MADRID • WARSAW • BUDAPEST • AUCKLAND

ISBN 0-373-03473-3

BRIDE ON THE RANCH

First North American Publication 1997.

This edition published by arrangement with Harlequin Books S.A.

® and TM are trademarks of the publisher. Trademarks indicated with
® are registered in the United States Patent and Trademark Office, the
Canadian Trade Marks Office and in other countries.

Printed in U.S.A.

PROLOGUE

MAGGIE Foster tried not to fidget under the disapproving gaze of the agency owner, but it became more difficult when the older woman's sharp eyes frowned so menacingly. Sarah Montgomery, owner, representative and chief factotum of the Montgomery Employment Agency, reviewed the file before her. Her iron gray hair drawn into a no-nonsense style suited her brusque personality. She dropped her gaze to the thin folder she had opened and scanned her notes.

"This is the third place that has fired you for daydreaming," she said severely.

Maggie swallowed hard and tried to think up a convincing answer that would get her one more chance. She needed a job. Clearing her throat, she smiled and nodded. "I admit I was...distracted, but only that one time."

Mrs. Montgomery raised an eyebrow and flicked a glance at the younger woman. "It says you mixed up the orders repeatedly. You burned the burgers, and your milkshakes were more milk than anything."

"I don't think a fast-food restaurant is exactly my kind of place," Maggie said with dignity.

"Miss Foster, I'm beginning to wonder if anything is your kind of place. We placed you with Bennett, Strife and Harwell as receptionist." She referred to the pages that sat on the left of the folder. "You mixed up the telephone messages, hung up on an important client, and were found daydreaming when the phones were ringing off the wall. When they fired you, we tried Markham's department store. You mixed up the sales register so badly I think they are still trying to straighten it out. You sent merchandise to the wrong address, and you ignored valued customers because you were daydreaming."

Maggie dropped her gaze. She didn't need Mrs. Montgomery reciting the litany. She knew her mind hadn't been on the jobs she'd held. She wanted to write. But until she could make a living from writing, she needed a way to earn money to live on. Thanks to her domineering father's edict that she prepare herself for an advantageous marriage, Maggie had not been trained for anything, except perhaps being the finest hostess in the state. Now that she had moved out on her own, she qualified for very little.

"This is the third job in two months," Mrs. Montgomery reiterated.

Maggie nodded. A touch of panic shot up her spine. If she didn't get something else right away she would be out of money. The last thing she wanted to do was return home and admit her father had been right.

"Can you cook?"

Maggie looked up, meeting Mrs. Montgomery's eyes. "Yes." She wasn't great by any means, but she could prepare plain meals.

"I have a possible position." For once Mrs. Montgomery permitted herself a small smile. "It might be a match made in heaven," she murmured to herself. "Or the fastest dismissal in the agency's records."

"For a cook?" Maggie asked.

"For a cook and housekeeper on a ranch outside town."

"I'll take it!"

Mrs. Montgomery obviously disapproved of her enthusiasm. She fixed her disapproving gaze once more on Maggie and shook her head slowly. "It's the last thing

I have for you, but it won't be easy. Kyle Carstairs is impossible to work for."

"I'm sure I can manage." Maggie Foster smoothed her palms over the plain blue skirt she'd worn for the interview. With the starched white blouse and red blazer, she hoped she looked the epitome of competency. She had fussed with her curly light brown hair that morning, taming it into a semblance of order. Her makeup was discreet. She needed this job.

"He's had five housekeepers in the last seven months. Four weeks was the longest anyone stayed." Sarah Montgomery's dour comments were no doubt intended to dissuade Maggie from pursuing the position. It had no effect.

"I'm sure I can manage." Maggie refused to dwell on the possibility that the agency would not send her. Her credentials were scarce, she had very little work experience, and what she had wasn't outstanding by any means. But she could make this assignment work. One way or another she planned to escape the life she'd known. And she now had a definite goal for her future. She would succeed! If the agency would give her the chance.

The older woman peered at Maggie over the frames of her half-glasses. If Mrs. Montgomery's intent was to intimidate, Maggie thought, she came close to succeeding. But Maggie would not let the older woman know it. Schooling her features to reflect a calm confidence she was far from feeling, Maggie returned her gaze. Anticipation simmered in her veins. She had to get the job. And she'd do it to the best of her ability.

"The ranch is over an hour's drive from Cheyenne."

Maggie nodded. That would suit her fine. She had no need to dash into town. A glimmer of excitement bubbled up inside her. Another chance. One she would not lose.

"From the reports of the housekeepers who worked there, Kyle Carstairs is bossy, arrogant, and quite demanding. Nothing pleases him."

Maggie took a deep breath. He sounded like her father, and Don. She had had years of experience dealing with men like that. Would taking this job be exchanging one tyrant for another?

"I've had experience dealing with that situation," she said calmly. She knew office work didn't suit her. Nor retail sales. Nor fast-food restaurants. Growing panicked, she crossed her fingers. She wanted this job.

The older woman studied her briefly, dropped her gaze back to the opened folder. "Very well. I'll call and let him know you are on your way." Reaching beside her, she handed a thick envelope to Maggie. "Directions to the Rafter C Terms and conditions of employment. If you have any questions, call me. Good luck, Miss Foster. You'll need it."

CHAPTER ONE

MAGGIE slowed her car to a stop near the large white ranch house. She had been on Rafter C land for several minutes, the drive from the road to the house had been over two miles in length. She surveyed her new home and work location as her fingers switched off the ignition. The two-story clapboard house charmed her. Could a man who owned it be all bad, as Mrs. Montgomery had hinted? Following the directions in the packet the agency had provided, she'd driven to the back of the house. Apparently the Carstairses didn't use the front door often. The porch that wrapped around three sides of the house stopped short of the back. Instead there was a single door, a small wooden stoop at the top of three steps, and tamped-down dirt for a yard. Beyond rose a huge barn, the gray paint a surprising change from the red she expected. The spanking-white trim sparkled in the early morning sun.

She had arrived in plenty of time to get settled before preparing lunch. Anxious to prove to her new boss that she was capable of the job, she had done her best to be prompt, and dressed to blend in.

She opened the car door and stepped out, a bit self-conscious. Her jeans were worn and comfortable, as was her cotton T-shirt. Only the boots were new. She didn't have a hat. Not that she planned to spend much time outside; her work was in the house. But a cowboy hat would have been the perfect touch.

Glancing around, Maggie noticed several men in and around the barn. One worked with a horse in the large corral, another sat on a turned-up barrel, a tangle of leather straps in his hand. Two others paused in their tasks as they stopped to watch her. A tall man came from inside the barn at the sound of her car. She shielded her eyes against the sun's glare with the palm of her hand and waited. Her heart thumped in her chest as she watched him approach.

She didn't believe in time travel, but suddenly wondered if she were wrong. He looked like a Viking. Tall, several inches over six feet, broad, blond, he strode across the dusty yard as if a conqueror returning home. His stride swiftly ate up the ground, smoothly, predatorially, triumphantly. He slapped his hat against his thigh, dislodging a speck of hay while the sun's rays burnished the thick blond hair like old Spanish doubloons. His eyes narrowed as he studied her, drawing closer every second.

Maggie took a deep breath and dropped her hand, her eyes fixed on him. Slowly a smile lit her face. Hero material was scarce. Yet right before her eyes stood the perfect specimen. Greedily her gaze traveled from his broad shoulders across his muscular chest to his slim waist, hips, muscular thighs. The jeans displayed his masculine attributes to perfection. The dusty boots encasing his feet completed the image.

She raised her eyes, anxious for a pen and paper to capture the sensations that jostled around inside, to capture for all time the decidedly feminine feelings that flooded her being, the unexpected delight she discovered in being female to his blatant masculinity. When her gaze reached his face, his scowling expression jolted her back to awareness of where she was, who she was.

"Lost?" he asked, setting the hat on his head, tilted down to shadow his eyes.

She shook her head and smiled again. The spiraling sense of anticipation that tantalized her shimmered unexpectedly. The urge to step closer, feel his heat, align herself with him, was totally foreign. Yet she found herself hard-pressed to resist.

"I'm Maggie Foster, your new housekeeper."

His look became incredulous as he trailed his gaze down her slim figure, pausing briefly at the shiny new boots. He shook his head as his eyes drifted back to hers.

"This some kind of joke?" he asked.

"No." Reaching into the car, she withdrew the employment packet and pulled Mrs. Montgomery's letter from the stack. "Mrs. Montgomery said she would be calling you."

Kyle Carstairs took the letter, scanned it briefly and looked at Maggie. What the hell was he supposed to do now? Mrs. Montgomery had called yesterday to inform him she'd found him yet another housekeeper. But she had neglected to mention the woman was young and pretty and totally unsuitable for the job. For heaven's sake, he could smell roses from where he stood.

His eyes traveled over her again. Too young. She had to be years younger than he. And far too feminine. She curved in all the right places, not that he cared. He'd sworn off women himself, but he didn't need the distraction she'd cause the men. Besides, she didn't look capable of staying the course. Probably some fluffy-headed woman who thought living on a ranch was all fun and games. Or was she looking to hook a rancher, like Jeannie?

What had the agency been thinking of? Just because he had had five housekeepers since Rachel left was no excuse to send this one. None of the others had been worth a damn. Yet each one of them offered more than this little slip of a woman could.

"Sorry you had the drive out, you won't do." He folded the letter and handed it back to Maggie.

Maggie blinked in shock. "What do you mean, I won't do? You haven't interviewed me, haven't seen me cook or clean. Besides, as I've heard it, you don't have much choice. I'm the best you've got right now." She would not let her opportunity flee. She slammed the car door and stepped closer to the man.

"Are you Kyle Carstairs?" she asked, making sure she was talking to the boss, not some foreman or flunky who thought to throw his weight around.

"Right. Boss of the Rafter C. Around here what I say goes, and I say you won't do."

Maggie glanced around as if looking for support. While the cowboys watched them, they had resumed their work. Turning back to face him, stepping closer, her fists on her hips, her chin jutting out belligerently, she wanted to scream, but settled for asking through clenched teeth, "And where are all the other housekeepers who are so much better than I? As I see it, Mr. Carstairs, you don't have anyone else." She knew this. He knew this. "Maybe you should consider giving me a try before throwing me off your ranch."

He reached out and took one of her fists, prying open the fingers and smoothing his thumb across the soft skin of her palm. Shivering as waves of sensation danced up her arm, Maggie was mesmerized by his totally unexpected touch.

"Working on a ranch is hard work. Your hands are too soft to have done anything even close to what's required here," Kyle said, his thumb moving in an erotic pattern back and forth.

Maggie tried to pull away, but his grip held firm. She glared at him. "I'm not here to do ranch work. I'm here to do housework. How hard do you think that is?"

"Harder than you're used to," he retorted.

She held his eyes with effort. He hit close to home, but she refused to acknowledge it. She found it difficult enough trying to think with her hand firmly held by his. Tempted to hold out her other hand so he could take it, as well, she drew in a deep breath, tried to rein her clamoring senses under some control.

"Who does the work now?" she asked.

He shrugged, his thumb still rubbing across her palm. His eyes dropped to the movement, as if mesmerized by the soft feel of her skin. Taking a deep breath, the gentle scent of roses that surrounded them filled his nostrils. "The men and I are making do until the next housekeeper arrives."

"Then your troubles are over. I've arrived. I'm her."

He shook his head.

"Normally—" She cleared her throat. What was normal about a man holding her hand? Nothing. Her heart pounded. Her skin tingled at his touch. Tugging, she freed herself and involuntarily stepped back. The glare in his steely gray eyes unnerved her. Yet she wanted this job more than anything. It was her last chance. She refused to meekly climb back into her car and head back to Cheyenne.

"Normally what?" he asked.

"Normally, do the men cook?"

"I had a housekeeper that had been here for years. When her mother became ill and needed her, she left. She's been gone for most of a year now. Normal changed when she left. One of these days the agency will send someone appropriate who will stay as long as Rachel did and the problem will go away."

Maggie smiled, hoping the insincerity didn't show. "I'm that person. Looks to me as if you don't have much choice. You've driven the rest away. The Montgomery Agency couldn't get anyone else, so you're stuck with me."

"Or I can go to another agency." He frowned at her, as if he disliked hearing the situation put into words.

"With the same results. Five housekeepers in seven months isn't a great track record it seems to me." Where were the words coming from? She never stood up to her father, how could she stand up to this giant of a man?

"And you'll do better? The longest any of them stayed was four weeks."

Maggie nodded. "I'll stay longer than four weeks. And be the best darn housekeeper you've ever had." She kept the smile plastered on her face, hoping he couldn't see how her heart raced.

Kyle didn't want her to stay. Here only ten minutes and she reminded him of his ex-fiancée, Jeannie. Not in looks. Jeannie had been tall and blond. This woman stood shorter, barely up to his chin, with light brown hair that waved as soft as silk around her face. For a split second temptation swept through him to brush his fingers through the waves to see if they were as soft as they looked. Clenching his hands into fists, he resisted the urge. Hormones had misled him before, he wouldn't go that route again. She was too young, too much temptation to keep around. He wanted a woman of fifty, with grown kids and a lifetime of keeping house. A woman like his mother, who relished ranch life, enjoyed cooking for the men and sharing in the conversation at dinner that centered on cattle, market price of beef, and rodeos. Not some flighty young thing that looked as if a puff of strong Wyoming wind would blow her away.

Yet she had a point, dammit. His house was a disaster. He hunted for clean clothes every day, hated doing laundry. His men were grumbling with the catch-as-catch-can cooking. One had quit last month, refusing to cook. Even Lance, his foreman, had grumbled and threatened to look for another job if he had to cook another meal. And not one of the over-fifty housekeepers that had come to work had stayed.

He was going to say yes, and live to regret it. He knew it. Yet she had clearly stated the situation, he desperately needed help. For however long she stayed, he could use the help. And he'd call the agency and tell them to continue looking.

"You can stay temporarily. But only until I get the agency to send someone more suitable," he conceded.

Maggie nodded and looked away, trying to hide her delight. She knew the agency wouldn't even look for a replacement while she remained in residence. And if she played her cards right, she'd do just fine until she finished her book. If it sold, then she could decide whether to stay until it became published or move back to town to write another one. There was plenty of time to decide that in the future. She had barely started. But the ideas crowded her brain. A dozen more sprang to mind from seeing Kyle Carstairs. With her own fertile imagination, and the quiet setting of the ranch to create, she should have the book she'd already started completed within a few weeks, a couple of months at the most. Then there would be no stopping her.

"Come on, I'll show you around the place. You can unpack and get lunch ready before starting anything else. There are ten ranch hands plus me and you. Can you cook for a crowd that size?"

"Sure." How hard could it be? She'd just multiply what she wanted to eat by twelve.

"We eat at six, one and seven. Sometimes later if we're branding or dipping."

She nodded, wondering what branding and dipping were, wondering why he'd had such a hard time getting anyone to stay. Three meals a day, even if one was at six in the morning, a quick flick of the dust cloth and the rest of the day would be hers. Of course, one or two days a week she would have to vacuum and do laundry, but aside from that there would be plenty of time available to write her book. She smiled. She was here now, and she wasn't budging.

Kyle's long stride quickly covered the distance between her car and the stoop at the back door. His boots rang loud on the wood as he skipped the second step and hit the third. Maggie hurried to keep up. She would show him—

Oops. Her slick boot sole slipped off the edge of the step. Flinging her arms out to try to avoid a fall, she encircled Kyle's thigh, slamming against him with her full weight. He lurched, unable to catch his balance because of her death grip, tumbling on the narrow porch with a loud thump. Maggie followed him down, crashing against him.

"Oh, no. I'm so sorry." Scrambling, Maggie knelt on the second-to-the-top step, her hand on his thigh. "Oh, Mr. Carstairs, are you all right? I'm so sorry." Ineffectively she patted his leg, wondering if she'd killed her new boss.

When he raised up on one elbow and glared at her, she knew she hadn't. Though maybe it might have been better for her if she had. Anger shone in his eyes; his body seemed to grow in stature.

"There are several steps there," he said through gritted teeth. "You are to take them one at a time."

"I know. I...my boot slipped."

He sat up and looked at her kneeling on the stair like a supplicant. "Trouble walking?" he growled sarcastically.

"It was an accident. Surely even the boss of the Rafter C has had an accident on occasion."

He rose, reached down to grasp her upper arm, and hauled her to her feet. Waiting until she stood on the stoop with him before releasing her, he muttered something under his breath.

"What?"

"Nothing." He took a deep breath. "Accidents do happen. Come on." Holding open the door, he ushered her into the large country kitchen.

It looked a mess. Dishes soaked in cold water, a thin film of congealed grease floating on top. Sugar gritted beneath her feet as she walked into the room. The windows were bare of curtains, the table needed wiping.

"Looks like I got here just in time," she said, hiding her dismay.

"I never said I didn't need anyone. Just, you won't do."

What was the man's problem? His disapproval was almost tangible, yet he didn't know her from Adam. Tilting her chin, Maggie silently vowed she would prove to be the best housekeeper he ever had. And when she sold her book and was ready to move on, he'd beg her to stay. He'd grovel at her feet for ever doubting her. And she'd turn up her nose at his blandishments and walk away without a backward glance. She'd show him she could "do."

"Pantry and freezer are through there." He pointed to a door on the side wall. "Might need some things. We've been too busy working on the fencing and tallies to mess much with shopping and such."

"That's what I'm here for. Why don't you go on back outside and do what you were doing and I'll get things settled here." Maggie didn't want him hanging around while she tried to bring some order out of this chaos. She knew she wasn't superwoman, but anyone with a lick of sense could at least clean up.

Then she'd see to the meals.

"Maggie Foster."

She swung around. "What?"

"Just verifying that's your name."

For a heartbeat she felt a tug of recognition. A pull of attraction. Which she immediately clamped down on.

She wanted no distractions in the form of some male. She had come to escape a domineering father who thought he had the right to run her life for her. She had come to forget her disastrous foray into love and establish herself in a new career. The last thing she wanted was to feel any attraction toward her new boss.

Not that she could totally ignore Kyle Carstairs, of course. He was her boss. And he was the perfect example of what a man should look like. She'd have to be dead to deny that. Not that she would let herself act upon it at all. She knew all about men. How they wanted women to wait on them hand and foot. How they derided any attempts to grow and develop. How they ignored her needs and used her for their own ends.

Now the tide had turned and she would use men. She would observe the cowboys on the ranch and use them in her book. She'd research what they liked and what they didn't. What better place for research than a ranch full of men? And it would be strictly research, no personal involvement. She would hold herself aloof and disdainful, taking what she needed, discarding the rest. She was not staying for life. Once her book sold, she'd move on.

"You all right?" Kyle asked, shaking her arm a little.

Blinking, Maggie nodded. "A bit daunted by the task ahead, but I can manage." She had to watch her daydreaming. He was too quick to let her slip away in her mind like she did so often. She didn't need that escape anymore. She had walked out of her father's house and life and had no intentions of ever returning.

He glanced around. "Wouldn't take Rachel long to clean this up."

"My guess is Rachel would never have let it get this bad," she replied tartly. "Don't you have work to do?"

"Miss Foster, in case you were wondering, I run this spread, not you."

"I never said I ran it. I'm just trying to ease you out the door so I can get to work. I don't need supervision."

She turned to face him. Big mistake. He stood too close, was too masculine. For the first time in ages Maggie wondered what she looked like. Had her lipstick worn off? Had the breeze in the yard tangled her hair? Did her clothes fit all right? Swallowing hard, she wished she dare move. Either a step back for safety's sake, or a step forward so she could feel his heat, breathe in the scent of him that she'd caught when they had tangled on the stoop.

"There will be five of us in for lunch. The rest of the men won't be back until supper. Can you manage?"

"Yes."

She watched him shake his head in doubt and head back outside. Breathing a sigh of relief, Maggie turned to the mess awaiting her. It didn't look as if she would be writing anything today. Once she cleaned up the kitchen, she would unpack, unload her computer and get it set up. At least she could do that much today.

By the time the men streamed in for lunch, Maggie had managed to clean the kitchen, or at least most of it. She had rummaged around in the cupboards and pantry and begun a list of food items to purchase to feed the crew at Rafter C. The supplies were limited. It was long past time someone went shopping. She'd done her best with lunch, but it was a pitiful array that met the eyes of the hungry cowboys.

Peanut butter and jelly sandwiches mingled with grilled cheese on two large platters in the center of the table. There were small bowls of canned soup: vegetable, beef barley and cream of mushroom. A huge pot of black coffee bubbled on the stove. At least there was plenty of that.

Kyle walked to the head of the table and stared at the platters. Slowly he raised his gaze to hers. The look of disbelief was blatant. "This is lunch?"

She nodded, suddenly wary. There was little food to be had. She'd done her best. But seeing his frown of disapproval, she instantly knew it wasn't enough.

The other men sank down in the chairs, silent as they surveyed the stacks of sandwiches, the bowls of mismatched soup. As one, they all looked at Maggie.

She smiled brightly. "I'm Maggie Foster." No one said a word. "The new housekeeper."

"Where did you work before, ma'am, at a kids' school?" one of the older men asked.

"Get started. I'll be back in a minute," Kyle said. Gripping Maggie's arm, he marched her from the room and down the hall to the room he used as his office. Slamming the door behind him, he spun her around until they faced each other. "Is lunch supposed to be a joke?" he asked. "Or is this your idea of being what I needed for a housekeeper? These are hardworking, hungry men. Not some ladies at a tea!"

Maggie felt like a fool and a failure. There had been limited supplies, but, granted, if she had been a true housekeeper, she would have known how to fix something else for hardworking men. Peanut butter and jelly suddenly seemed childish, and not very filling. But once she had finished washing all the dirty dishes, there had not been much time to prepare a full-blown meal, not with food readily available. The heat of his anger washed through her. Blinking in surprise, she stood her ground, a matching anger beginning to build.

"It's no joke. It's all I found to feed this crew. If you want to eat better you should buy more food!"

"So do we expect hot dogs for dinner?"

She ignored his scathing tone and shook her head. "I have time to go into town and get some food for dinner."

"All the men will be in for dinner, that's ten plus you and me. You told me you could manage to feed that many; having second thoughts?" What the hell was he doing, offering her a second chance? He'd been mad clear through when he first saw the skimpy platter of sandwiches. Yet now she looked so determined, meeting his gaze bravely, he had a hard time holding on to anger. He was not getting soft with some stranger, no matter how pretty! "These men engage in hard physical labor all day long. We need a lot of food to keep us going. And we prefer something with a bit more substance than peanut butter."

"You had it in the cupboard, I assumed it was to be used," she snapped back. She knew she'd blown it. But there had not been a big choice of food. At least everyone had eaten.

"Probably for Rachel, or one of the other house-keepers. I don't remember being served peanut butter and jelly sandwiches since my mother died."

She stood tall and nodded. "I stand corrected. In future I'll make sure there are ham and cheese and roast beef sandwiches." She gritted her teeth lest the words tumbling around spilled out. So she had a bit to learn. She could do it. And it would help if there were some food around to prepare. She'd stock up the kitchen with so much food there would always be choices for the meals.

"The grilled cheese sandwiches were a good idea. I hope there are one or two left when we get back in there."

"If there had been more cheese or bread, I would have fixed more. Your pantry is practically bare, your refrigerator has more green stuff growing in it than your yard, and the freezer holds sides of cows, not nice little packets that could be quickly thawed and used."

"If you can't do the job—"

She whirled around and stormed away in anger. Was that his out, fire her after one meal? She wasn't going to give in easily over this. She needed this job. And he needed a housekeeper. She turned to face him, feeling braver with the distance of the room between them. "I just got here a couple of hours ago. I needed to shovel out the dirt you had accumulated in that kitchen over the last few weeks, then scrounge around for food to feed over half a dozen people. I'm a writer, not a magician. I can't clean off enough plates to eat from and conjure up food all with a wave of my hand. I did just fine for what raw materials I had to work with. Once I get some shopping done, I'll manage fine!"

"A writer?" Kyle repeated, picking up on the word. "You're a writer?"

She closed her eyes briefly. Stupid! She hadn't wanted anyone to know until she sold a book. Not after the mocking comments of her father and Don.

"I thought you were a housekeeper. You're a writer?" Kyle asked suspiciously.

She opened her eyes and glared at him. "What I do in my off time is my business. Your house won't suffer because I write."

"What do you write?" If she was a reporter set on a story, he'd kick her off the ranch so fast the new would rub off her boots.

"Books," she mumbled, her gaze dropping to his throat. She watched his pulse, fascinated to see its slow, steady beat against the hollow of his throat. She longed to touch it, to see if she could feel the pulsing blood, feel—

"What kind of books?"

She didn't need this. She didn't need the laughter and derision she'd find. But she was no stranger to it. Her own father laughed at her ideas. Her ex-fiancé had scoffed at her ambitions. But she firmed her resolve, refusing to allow her father, ex-fiancé or new boss to deter her.

"Romance novels," she said proudly.

CHAPTER TWO

"WHAT?" Kyle took a step closer, his eyes blazing down at Maggie. "You've come here to write love stories? Or is it research you are interested in? Stay away from my ranch hands! I don't want you doing any kind of *romance* research here. The first thing I know, I'll have a mutiny on my hands. You're here to act as housekeeper. Damn, I should send you packing now."

"My imagination is much better than reality. Anyway, I have it on good authority that I'm not so hot in the romance department. I don't plan to seduce any of your men. Does that make you feel better?" She turned away, aware of the heat in her cheeks. She knew she was beet red, and didn't need any more embarrassment. She also knew she should not have mentioned romance books. Men all thought—

"No writing on my time."

"I will do my best on this job, you don't need to worry, Mr. Carstairs. I have never..." She trailed off. She had planned to say she had never had a problem with her work, but that wasn't strictly true. Her father constantly berated her for less than the perfection he sought. Her attempts to work in an office and the department store in the mall had met with far less than perfect results. Even the fast-food place had fired her. Scrupulously honest, Maggie could not tell Kyle Carstairs she never did less than outstanding work.

He didn't seem to notice her lapse. "Call me Kyle," he growled, heading for the door. "And see that you do your best."

He whipped it open and in seconds Maggie was alone. Slowly, she followed. The kitchen was empty. Crumbs on the plates indicated the men had eaten the sandwiches. She wondered if they had left anything for Kyle. He must have grabbed something or she was sure she would have heard about it. She wished they had left her half a sandwich at least. Maggie cleared the rest of the table and did the dishes as her mind endlessly played over the scene in the study. She would do a good job for Kyle Carstairs, she vowed. But *she* would decide how to spend her free time. And she wanted to write books, love stories.

After the scathing remarks her ex-fiancé Don had made about her own abilities to attract and hold a man, she didn't think she would ever fall in love again, nor attract anyone to her. When he'd asked her to marry him, she had thought him a perfect mate. But her kisses didn't meet his standards; her own reluctance to go to bed before their marriage had confirmed his own belief that she had little sex appeal, and less attraction. Even now, seven months later, the pain of his words pierced sharp and direct.

So, facing reality, as her father constantly insisted, she knew better than to hope to find a man interested in her as a female. Thinking she could appease her romantic nature by writing a book, a love story that would satisfy her own desires for a happy ending and offer some reading pleasure to others, she had started.

Of course, while she had her imagination, she needed to draw some information from others. Her own experience was extremely limited. Maybe she could cleverly work the questions she had into conversations with the cowboys on the Rafter C. Maybe they could clue her in to what men really wanted in a mate, what they liked about women, beyond the obvious, and what they disliked about relationships. She had plenty of material on what she as a woman disliked, from Don. And even her father. Enough to start, not enough to give her book the in-depth feeling she longed for.

The kitchen at last set to rights, she wiped her hands on the damp dish towel, tossed it on the counter and headed for the door. There was not enough food in the place for dinner. If she was to shop for the evening meal, she had better get going. Time was short, and the distance to the nearest town considerable.

She headed to the barn, searching for Kyle. How did she buy the food? Did he have a charge account at the local store, or did he have to give her cash for the purchases? She had a list, of sorts. Hopefully she had remembered everything she would need over the next few days. She didn't have much experience in preplanning meals. It hadn't been important before. Her father always had a cook.

The wind blew from the west, tossing her hair around her face, and bringing with it a mingled scent of horses, cattle, grass and fresh air. Maggie took a deep breath, held it to savor the freshness. As she reached the barn, the fragrance of hay became strong. She liked the blended aromas, good and bad. They were a far cry from downtown Denver and automobile fumes.

"Can I help you, little lady?" One of the older cowboys came out from the tack room. Maggie recognized him immediately as the one who had asked if she'd worked in a kindergarten. Her smile was hesitant.

"Actually, I'm looking for Mr. Carstairs. Kyle. I need to go shopping for some food and don't know where he likes to shop or how to pay for the food."

"Kyle's out somewhere. The Rafter C has an account at the Shop 'N Shop on the edge of town. Cheyenne. Talk to the manager before you shop and he'll ring it up on Kyle's tab. All the housekeepers did that."

"Thanks. I'll be back for dinner." Smiling, she turned back to her car. If she had only known they needed food before she had arrived, she could have shopped on her way to the ranch, rather than heading back to Cheyenne the same day.

She backed her car around and turned toward the drive just as Kyle rode up. Pausing until he passed her, she watched as he sat on the big bay horse like he'd been born to the saddle, tall and easy, his long legs hugging the horse's sides. She couldn't help staring. Whether he wanted it or not, whether he ever found out or not, he was going to be the role model for the hero of her book. Maybe not his personality—she wanted a kinder, gentler man. But his face was perfect, rough-hewn, taut and tanned. She wished he didn't wear a hat. She would like to see the golden glow of his thick, wavy hair in the sunlight again. His shoulders gave the impression they could carry the weight of the world. Some woman would be lucky to have him shoulder her burdens one day. His hands were strong and capable. Capable of being tender, she acknowledged as she remembered his thumb rubbing gently across her palm. And capable of bringing an awareness that didn't end. Her heart rate sped up at the memory of his hand holding hers.

Kyle did not pass. He reined in and dismounted in one fluid motion right beside her. Maggie rolled down the window when he leaned over her car.

"Leaving?" His voice was silky with satisfaction.

"Only to buy groceries. I'll be back for dinner," she replied sweetly, giving him a false smile when she seethed with frustration. She didn't understand why he wanted her to leave so much. She would have thought he would be so grateful to have someone do the housework and cooking, he would make an effort to appease that person. Her. She wanted him to ask her to stay. To do something to show that she was special to him, if only to relieve him of the tasks around the house.

Special to him? She didn't want to be special to anyone. She wanted to prove to herself and her father that she was capable of choosing her own life and living it the way she wanted. Maybe one day, in the far distant future, she would find a man who would love her for herself, not for her sexiness, which she obviously lacked, not because she waited on him hand and foot. But just because of who she was.

And it was certain that that man would be nothing like Kyle Carstairs. Though, she sighed softly, in all honesty he probably would not approach Kyle in the looks department. Kyle had to be the best-looking male she'd ever seen.

"What are you getting?"

"Do you want to see the list?" She snatched it up from the seat beside her and thrust it through the open window. Kyle made no move to take it. His eyes glimmered as he stared down through the window. Shaded by his hat, they appeared as cool as a frosty foggy morning. But Maggie had seen them flare hot and silver when angry.

"So you're coming back?" he asked.

"Yes! Honestly, do you think to drive me away with your attitude? You need me."

"And you're just a girl who wants to be needed."

Was that part of the attraction of staying in a job where her boss obviously didn't want her? She wanted to be needed for the first time in her life?

She pulled her hand back, tossed the list beside her and put the car in gear. "I have work to do. As boss you can laze around if you want, but if I'm to get back in time to make dinner, I need to get going."

His teeth were white and even when he smiled at her saucy speech. Maggie took a deep breath and forced her eyes forward. Time enough later to build up resistance, if they wanted dinner at seven, she had to hurry.

Kyle stood back and watched as Maggie maneuvered her car around the house and drove back down the driveway. A snippy thing; none of his other housekeepers sassed him like she did. He must be getting soft in the head, he allowed it. Next time he'd remind her of the respect due the boss of a spread the size of the Rafter C. Remind her she was only here temporarily, and if she wanted to stay even until the next housekeeper arrived, she had better watch her mouth.

It took Maggie much longer to find the store than she had planned. And buying everything on her list from a supermarket that was totally unfamiliar took even longer. Consequently, by the time she reached the Rafter C, it would be close to the dinner hour. Even then, she was pushing it.

She stopped at a take-and-bake pizza parlor and bought three large pizzas. Surely cowboys loved pizza. And living so far from town, they probably didn't get it often. As soon as she reached home, she would pop them in the oven while she unloaded her car. By the time she had the groceries inside, the pizzas would be ready to serve. She wouldn't have time to prepare more. There were a lot of perishable groceries she would have to put away at once. Tomorrow she'd fix a full meal with a roast, baked potatoes, vegetables and biscuits.

Arriving at the Rafter C, Maggie felt a warm glow around her heart. It almost felt as if she were coming home. She hadn't even taken her suitcases from her car, yet the homestead welcomed her back as if she'd lived there for years.

No sooner had she stopped near the back door than Kyle strode out of the house. He opened the passenger door and began to pull out grocery bags. Maggie carried the pizzas inside and turned on the oven. The double ovens would come in handy, she'd be able to cook all the pizzas at once.

"Took you long enough," he said as he dumped two bags on the long counter.

"I had trouble finding the right store. Then I had to wait while the manager finished talking with a sales rep to get the okay to charge the purchases. And then there was a lot to buy." She headed back to unload other bags from her car, Kyle at her side. Had he helped the other housekeepers? She didn't ask. It was enough that he helped her.

When the groceries had been unloaded, Kyle reached in the trunk for her two suitcases. "I'll take these to your room. It's at the top of the stairs on the right. Did you see it when looking over the house this morning?" he asked.

"Actually, I didn't have a chance to look over the place, I was too busy cleaning the kitchen. Just dump them inside the door, I'll find them after dinner." If she were sleeping upstairs on the right, where did he sleep? Not in the bunkhouse, of that she was sure. She had not given the sleeping arrangements any thought. Not that it mattered. She was more than sure Kyle Carstairs could contain his lust around her.

She quickly put up the frozen packages and the milk. The rest could wait until after dinner. Hurrying to set the table, Maggie wanted everything to be ready when the men trooped in. She refused to give Kyle anything to complain about.

Promptly at seven, Kyle walked into the kitchen just as a stream of cowboys entered from the back door. Maggie wondered if there were a whistle somewhere that blew to let them know when mealtime arrived. They each introduced themselves. Maggie tried hard to remember what name went with which face.

She drew the pizzas from the ovens and set them on the big table. Finding a sharp knife, she handed it to one of the younger cowboys—was his name Billy?—and asked him to start cutting. Then she offered ice tea, coffee, and milk for beverages.

The men were silent as they ate. In only moments the pizzas were gone. They looked at her. Maggie looked around. She had not gotten a single piece. The silence stretched out and her eyes flew to Kyle. He leaned back in his chair, his fingers tucked into the front pockets of his jeans, his legs sprawled out before him as her eyes tracked her.

"Is something wrong?" she asked.

"No. We're just waiting for the rest," Kyle said slowly, the glimmer of a smile touching his lips, his gray eyes narrowed as he watched her. Curious to know what she would do. Give up and leave? Or had she more stamina than that?

"The rest?" Maggie's heart dropped. A quick glance around the table assured her she had not misread the situation. There had not been enough food. Again.

She swallowed. There was nothing else for dinner. She had thought several slices of pizza would be enough. She never ate more than two herself. God, what was she going to do? No one said a word, they all just stared at her. Panicked, she looked at Kyle again. Her job depended on her doing the work to his satisfaction. On providing good service. Not on sending cowboys to bed hungry.

A painful blush started in her chest and spread to her neck, her cheeks. The heat swamped her as the moments stretched out endlessly, silently. She swallowed again, praying for a miracle.

It came when Kyle shook his head and pushed back his chair. "Omelets. And biscuits. You can make biscuits, can't you?"

She nodded.

Kyle opened the industrial-size refrigerator and tallied the eggs. "Jason, go to the bunkhouse and see how many eggs you have there. We have two dozen here, bring back two dozen more if you have that many. Is there any meat?"

"There's some ham left over from the other night," one of the men volunteered.

"Bring that, too," Kyle ordered, already removing the eggs from the refrigerator.

Four dozen eggs? Maggie was astonished. Then reason quickly took over. Of course, there were a dozen people to feed and she already knew these men ate more than she did. Lots more. She should have figured that out on her own, especially after lunch. She moved to clear an area on the counter, and hunted for the flour. She would make enough biscuits for each man to have a dozen. She would—

"Carl, you and Pete put away the groceries. Trevor, you find the onions and cut them up. Jack grate cheese. Lance—"

"I'll take care of the coffee and condiments, boss," Lance interrupted, his eyes dancing in amusement. He cleared the trash from the pizzas and moved to the stove. "Dennis will hunt up some more vegetables and Steve can find the jam."

Reaching around Maggie, the cowboy called Lance drew down the large bags of flour. "It won't take long, ma'am, to know how much we like to eat. The pizza was a good idea, there just wasn't enough. We could probably each eat a whole one," he said gently.

Kyle glared at him and nodded toward the stove. Lance smiled, touched his forehead with two fingers in a mock salute and moved slowly away.

Maggie wished the floor would open up and take her away, but at least she had something to do and the men hadn't complained about having to do their own cooking. Though she knew they must be mad as hornets. They had worked hard all day and come to dinner expecting a hot meal. She'd fed them tidbits. Now they had to make their own suppers.

She darted a quick glance at Kyle. He had not said a word of reproach. In fact he seemed to be surprisingly calm about the entire episode. Yet she knew it would be reason enough to fire her. More than enough after lunch. No sense in waiting for the replacement that wouldn't come. He had enough incompetence to last.

Maggie ignored the rough teasing and laughter the men shared. She concentrated on making the biscuits, watching each batch cook to make sure they turned out perfect. She wanted to make amends, but wasn't sure how to do so. Wanted to prove she could do this job, but wasn't sure she'd get another chance. Kyle seemed a hard man, not one given to forgiving repeated errors in judgment.

When the omelets had been cooked and the first two batches of biscuits were on the table, the men sat down. Kyle came across the room and placed his hands on her shoulders, turning her from watching the stove to push her toward the chair next to his.

"We have timers for that. Sit down and eat."

She shook her head. "I'm fine. I wanted to make sure the biscuits were cooked." She didn't deserve his kindness. She'd made a mess of dinner.

His hands pushed her down into the chair. They were warm and hard, and when he removed them, she felt a chill. He sat at the head of the table and nodded toward her plate, which had been piled high with a fluffy cheese, ham and vegetable omelet. One of the men tossed a hot biscuit on the plate and another poured her a cup of coffee.

"Eat," Kyle ordered.

"Mrs. Montgomery said you were bossy," she muttered as she reached for some butter.

"She's got you pegged, boss," Lance said, giving a slow smile across the table to Maggie. "What else did the employment agency say? We know Kyle is hell on wheels with housekeepers. He hasn't kept one for longer than a couple of weeks."

Maggie looked up, tempted to relate all Sarah Montgomery had said, but she held her tongue. Kyle was her boss and deserved her loyalty. She smiled and shook her head. "Just that he was bossy. Which makes sense since he is the boss, right?"

"You could add slave driver," Carl mumbled, his eyes on his plate.

"Or stubborn," Dennis threw in.

"How about opinionated?" Jack said slyly, throwing Kyle a knowing look.

"I like relentless, myself," Pete said.

"And I like it quiet at dinner," Kyle said, frowning.

When everyone laughed, Maggie knew the men really liked and respected her new boss. It said a lot for him that the cowboys were comfortable enough around him to tease him. Something inside her reacted. She knew she still had to answer for the poor dinner, but maybe Kyle would be generous and give her one more chance. She would not repeat the mistake of too little food again.

As the men ate, conversation centered on the ranch and the different tasks and chores still to be done.

Maggie tried to match names to faces. Lance was the foreman. A man about the same age as Kyle, he maintained just enough distance from the men to keep the chain of command, yet from the easy way the others related, he obviously was also well liked.

Jack was older, his hair liberally sprinkled with gray. Billy was the youngest and looked to Maggie like he should still be in school. The others ranged in age and

size, yet all had the same undefinable characteristic of
the cowboy, a bit wild, a bit untamed, men in their own
right who signed on to work the open land as thcir fore-
bears had done a hundred years before.

Maggie found them fascinating. She soaked up the
conversation like a sponge. Afraid to ask questions, she
tried to glean the meaning from everything without ap-
pearing stupid. Once or twice someone explained things
to her, but for the most part she had to guess at the
meanings of some words.

When everyone had their fill of food and conversation, they began to drift out. Kyle left early and Maggie
wasn't sure whether to be glad or not. At least her rep-
rimand would be delayed, or had he gone to write a check
for her services and fire her? She hadn't done much her
first day. She hoped there would be more time. She
cleaned up the kitchen, checked where the cowboys had
stored the food and tried to plan the next day's menu.
Obviously she had not bought enough food to last a
week. But she had plenty for the next couple of days.
The first thing she planned to do when she hooked up
her computer was make a list of groceries, of meals, of
snacks. Then she would have a better idea of quantity
amounts to order.

Finished with the dishes, she headed toward the stairs
to find her room and unpack. At least she thought she
should unpack. Kyle still hadn't talked to her. But she
still didn't know where to find him. If he planned to fire
her, she was sure he would have done so immediately
after dinner. Or even as they were preparing the meal.

She paused in the doorway, her eyes taking in the
pretty room. It was large, with high ceilings. On the far
wall, tall windows gave a spectacular view of the rolling
fields. Starched Priscilla curtains framed the view. Slowly
she stepped inside. The bed was to one side, a dark bur-
gundy coverlet adding a splash of color against the white

walls. The rug in the center of the room gave beneath her feet when she walked on it. She would be very comfortable here. It was much more than she would have expected as a housekeeper.

As she opened drawers in the high chest, she wondered which room was Kyle's. Hers was at the top of the stairs. There was a door opposite, and three more farther down the hall. Time enough to discover his, when she was cleaning.

Maggie put away the last shirt, snapped closed her two bags and shoved them under her bed. Turning, she heard Kyle's tread on the stairs. Her door stood open so she could catch him if he came upstairs. She crossed her room, reaching the opening to the hall just as he reached the top of the stairs.

He looked tired. Yet when he saw her waiting, he straightened and raised one eyebrow.

"Thought you might be asleep by now. Breakfast is at six."

"I thought I might be fired by now."

He stared at her for a long moment. "No need. You're here temporarily. As soon as the agency finds someone else, you'll be gone. As you pointed out, I might as well take advantage of what you can do in the next few days."

"I plan on pancakes for breakfast, about fifteen for each man. Will that hold you?" she asked, disappointed by his conviction she would be so soon gone. Though in all fairness she had hardly impressed anyone today.

He smiled and nodded. "Probably."

"I'm sorry I made such a mess with dinner. I thought two or three slices of pizza would be enough. I won't make that mistake again."

"Something else, no doubt," he murmured. His gaze roamed over her face, her hair.

"No doubt." She grinned. He was being nicer than she expected.

"Where d'you get the pizzas?"

"At a take-and-bake place near the supermarket. I was running late and thought they'd do."

"They let you charge it?"

She shook her head. "I bought them."

Kyle studied her for a long moment. "How much experience do you have being a housekeeper?" he asked, moving to lean against the wall, crossing his arms over his chest. Maggie knew he would stay for a while, so there was no hope a quick answer would turn him away.

Leaning against the doorjamb, she put her hands in her pockets and tried to find an answer that would be truthful, yet give him the comfort he needed to know she could do the job.

"I kept house for a number of years," she began slowly.

"For a dozen men?"

She shook her head. "Just one, actually. Though we often had guests."

"Your dad?"

She nodded.

"Where is he now?" Kyle's eyes narrowed as she fidgeted in the doorway.

Maggie felt the subtle change from polite questioning to inquisition. She wanted to say good-night and shut the door, but couldn't without raising suspicions she wanted to avoid.

"He lives in Denver."

"Why did you take this job?"

Dare she hint at the reason? He probably sympathized with her father. He reminded her of her father, yet he was different. She didn't think her father would have come up with a plan for the evening meal when she failed to deliver. He would have sat back, waited for her to come up with something, then lectured her for hours on how inept she was. Kyle had not said a word. She almost wished he would. His kindness sat uneasily upon her. Boiling anger she was used to, kindness she was not.

Kyle counted the minutes as she stalled, obviously searching for some answer to appease him. For a moment anger flared. He didn't want to be fobbed off with some politically correct response, he wanted to know why she was working as a housekeeper on a ranch miles from anything when she should be in some town, building a career, dating. Frowning, he found he didn't like the idea of her dating, which was totally illogical. He didn't want to become involved with her or any woman. He'd tried that route with Jeannie, and look at the heartache that had caused.

Nothing good came of women practising their guile on unsuspecting men. He had a ranchful of single men, and he didn't need some pretty young woman causing havoc with her wiles. The sooner she left, the better.

"If it takes you as long to think up a plot for your book, you're going to be an old lady before you get the first manuscript done," he drawled sarcastically. Pushing away from the wall, he started down the hall.

"Get some sleep, 6:00 a.m. comes early," he called over his shoulder.

When he entered the farthest door on the left, Maggie sagged in relief. At least she'd made it through the first day. Slowly she entered her room and shut her door. She was an idiot. Now that the moment had passed she realized she should have had all her answers ready. Why would someone want to keep house at the back of beyond? She didn't ride particularly well, nor care for horses that much. She knew nothing about cattle. And she knew even less about men.

But she planned to remain for the duration. Tomorrow she'd get the house organized, set up her computer and begin working again on her book. In the meantime she would go to bed like Kyle suggested and forget about the less than enthusiastic welcome she'd received.

And ignore the shimmers of attraction that played between them. He was her boss for the foreseeable future, nothing more. She was happy to keep things that way. Not that it would hurt to just imagine how he would talk to her if he cared something for her. Not that it would hurt to just imagine how his skin would feel beneath her fingertips, how his mouth would feel against hers, how his arms would feel around her. Shivering, she shook her head. It would not hurt, but it wouldn't change anything. If anything, she needed to be practical now. Her future rested on it.

By the time a dozen people had eaten breakfast, Maggie was almost ready for a nap. She had risen early to prepare the meal, had everything ready when the ranch hands filed in. And she'd done it right. There was plenty of food for everyone, pancakes, sausages, even a couple of eggs fried for Jack when he asked. But the kitchen would take an hour or more to set right, and she still had to explore the rest of the house and make sure it was tidy before she could set up her computer. Conscientious, she knew she had to give her first efforts to her job. Her own time and projects had to wait.

She had lunch to see to and dinner to plan. Sipping from a cup of lukewarm coffee, she wondered where all the free time was she had expected. At the rate she was going, it would be the weekend before she even unloaded the computer from her car.

Determined to give her best to the job, however, Maggie didn't hesitate to plunge right in. Once the kitchen was clean, she wandered through the downstairs rooms. On the wall in the big living room, family pictures clustered. She studied them. They showed a happy family frolicking in the snow, on a picnic somewhere, on horseback, mother, father, three children. Then only pictures of the children. She noted the progression as they all grew up. The most recent pictures showed new family groups. Obviously Kyle's brother and sister were now starting families of their own. Why hadn't Kyle married?

As if her thoughts of him conjured him up, he appeared in the arch to the hall.

"What are you doing?" he asked, tapping his hat against his thigh as he studied Maggie's guilty expression when she whirled from the pictures.

"Just looking around. This room needs a thorough cleaning," she answered hurriedly. She didn't want him to know she'd been paying so much attention to a family that meant nothing to her.

But the pictures had tugged at her heart. She had been an only child of a difficult man. Her mother had left when she was a toddler, and her father had never spent time on picnics or playing with her in the snow. Kyle had been lucky in his childhood and for a moment envy crowded Maggie.

CHAPTER THREE

"THE whole place needs a thorough cleaning," he said, glancing around the room.

Maggie nodded and stepped forward. He was tall. If she used him as the hero in her book, she should probably know exactly how tall he stood. Stepping closer, she noticed her head just reached his chin. His shoulders seemed even broader when she came near like this. Her hands itched to measure the width, to feel the hardness of his muscles, to sculpt their strength.

Tilting her head slightly, she wondered how hot his skin would feel. Would it be sleek and taut over his muscles, or was his skin covered in hair? Golden hair covered his forearms, shining against the tan of his skin. Was he covered all over, or was his chest smooth and bare?

Swallowing hard, Maggie tried to move her gaze away from the man. While her perusal was for research, she found herself heating up at the thoughts running through her mind. Slowly she drew in a shaky breath and tried to remember what she was supposed to be doing.

"Are you all right?" Kyle's sharp voice penetrated the haze and she swung around to face him.

"Of course."

"You look as if you've gone into a trance."

"I was thinking of something for my story."

He leaned forward a little until he was close enough that his breath brushed against her cheek when he exhaled. Entranced, Maggie longed to reach up and touch his cheek, to trace the indentation beside his mouth, rub

41

her fingertip across his lips and see if they were soft and warm, or hard and cool.

"I want a full day's work for a full day's pay," he said.

She blinked. "Whyever would you think you wouldn't get it from me? I'm a hard worker."

"You've been here twenty-four hours and so far you have practically starved us and done nothing else," he replied.

She grew indignant. How dare he malign her efforts. "I cleaned your kitchen and went shopping for food, don't forget. Both were, I might add, a monumental task."

"Right, and by the amount of food you bought, you'll be heading out again tomorrow."

"Wait a minute. I wasn't aware of how much you would all eat. If you will recall, Mr. Carstairs, I offered to show you the list when I was leaving. If you had even glanced at it, you might have seen I was a little light on some of the supplies and let me know. So if I do have to go back tomorrow, I count you as much to blame as me."

Kyle stared at her in disbelief. "You're blaming me for your own ineptitude?"

She tilted her chin, planted her fists on her hips and nodded. "Not that I consider myself inept, just a bit inexperienced. Which you should have known."

"My dear Miss Foster, I expect the agency to send me someone competent and capable, not someone who has to be led around like a two-year-old."

Glaring at him, she wanted to stamp her foot at his arrogance.

"Hardly a two-year-old. As soon as I get my computer hooked up, I'll make a big list and be sure to buy more than enough of everything I need the next time I go shopping." A thought struck her. "But how I'll fit it all in my car, I'm not sure..." She trailed off. Her car had been packed with groceries yesterday. If she bought even more, she'd need to make two trips.

"Take one of the ranch trucks. You can fill the pickup bed with the groceries. That's what the other house-keepers did."

She frowned. "I don't know if I can drive a truck."

"It's almost like a car. I'll get one of the men to show you how if you don't think you can manage."

"I'm sure I can manage." Her tone was haughty, her eyes still flashed anger.

"I'm sure you can."

His gentle tone grated. Dropping her gaze, she watched his lips move as he talked, and oddly wondered how they would feel against her own. She had been kissed by Don numerous times, but she had not particularly liked it. Yet all the romance books she read made kisses sound like a most wonderful experience. Would Kyle's kisses be wonderful? Or sloppy wet and disgusting, like Don's?

He had shaved that morning, and his skin looked smooth and warm. If he kissed her, would she feel more of his face against her own than just his lips? Would his arms encircle her to pull—

"Maggie!"

She jumped. "What?"

He put a gentle fist beneath her jaw and raised her face until she met his gaze. His eyes narrowed as he stared down at her in displeasure, his expression serious.

"Do you need to go back to bed?"

To bed? With Kyle? She blinked again and tried to dispel the image his words evoked. She had never been to bed with a man. Don had tried for weeks, but she had refused. Glad now that she had, nonetheless she wondered a bit what it would be like. And with Kyle it would be gloriously different than with Don, of that she was sure.

"Why would I need to go to bed?" Was he propositioning her? She had to refuse. Didn't she?

He groaned softly and his fist opened. His hand cupped her chin and the pad of his thumb traced the soft skin covering her jaw.

Maggie shivered and leaned forward a millimeter. She liked his touch. Her skin transmitted the sensuous sensations throughout her entire body and shimmering tingles of awareness rushed through. She had never felt like this before. Could she capture this feeling in her book, too?

"Maggie, you look at me like I'm a long-awaited Christmas present. If you're making a play for me, forget it. I'm not interested. If this is research for your damn book, find someone else to practice on."

She jerked her head away and stepped back, embarrassment flooding her. "You told me to leave your employees alone."

"More importantly, leave me alone."

"I didn't do anything," she protested, knowing her imagination had been in full force but he couldn't know that. Could he?

"I guess not." He straightened, slapped his hat against his thigh again and looked around the room, as if surprised to find himself there. "I came in to do paperwork. You need to tell me how much the pizzas cost. I'll reimburse you."

"No need. It is the least I can do after making such a mess of things yesterday."

"You don't need to buy us food."

"I don't mind."

"Maggie, I pay for the food."

"All right! The receipt is in my purse, I'll get it when I finish cleaning here."

"Fine. I have some laundry that needs doing, too."

"Of course, I'm here to serve," she muttered, feeling the air in the room suddenly diminish. She needed to be alone to bring her rioting imagination under some control.

"Just so you remember."

"What?"

"That you're here to serve. Not to go off on some writing tangent any time you feel the urge."

Writing wasn't the urge she felt just now. Hitting him over the head with a vase came close. She tossed her hair and moved past him. "I know what I'm here for, and don't think I won't do the best job you've ever seen."

"You have a way to go to prove that to me," he mumbled, slamming his hat on his head and striding across the hall to the office.

Maggie almost acknowledged he had a point. So far her performance had not been very good. But she knew more now and wouldn't make the same mistakes twice.

She ran upstairs. While she cleaned the downstairs, she'd pop his things into the washer. Hesitating only a moment, she pushed open the door to his room. Glancing around curiously, Maggie studied the masculine clutter. Clothes were piled haphazardly around. The bed, rumpled and unmade, drew her attention. For a moment she imagined Kyle stretched out on the dark sheets, a golden warrior resting before the next battle. Sunlight bright and bold bathed the room in clear light. She moved to the piles of clothes and began to sort them for the wash. She could smell horses and dust and male sweat. Her heart kicked into high gear at Kyle's scent. Strong, masculine, enticing, it kept her attention focused on him even when he was absent.

Frowning, she picked up the pile of jeans and headed downstairs. The washer and dryer were off the kitchen. She'd start the load, and begin to clean the living room.

*   *   *

Just maybe this job wasn't the perfect one to enable her to write, Maggie admitted as she stood out of the way of the lunch stampede. She had made thick roast beef sandwiches for the men, three large ones each. A huge fruit salad, which had taken every bit of fruit she'd bought just yesterday, and three bags of chips graced the table, as well. She poured hot coffee as they began to eat.

Kyle arrived a couple of minutes after the rest of them and flicked a glance to Maggie as she scanned the table to make sure she'd prepared enough food this time.

"Coffee?" she asked as he sat at the head.

"Yes."

Kyle sipped the hot beverage and stared at her over the rim of the cup. Flushed from the heat in the kitchen, Maggie met his gaze, her eyes locked with his and she smiled shyly before turning away. He watched her cross the room, his gaze drifting down to the tight jeans that hugged her hips and her long legs. He set his cup down with a thunk and glanced around at the men eating. Lance met his eye, looked back at Maggie. Kyle frowned; he didn't need any of the men getting distracted by Maggie. He stared at Lance until the foreman met his gaze again and grinned.

Kyle didn't need the distraction himself. Maggie was his housekeeper until the agency sent another. Why they'd sent her in the first place was beyond him. And he didn't like it one bit. He wanted someone more suitable to ranch life. When Maggie sat down beside him and reached for a sandwich, he couldn't help noticing how gracefully she moved, how her hair gleamed in the kitchen light with threads of gold mingled with the brown. How her gaze moved shyly around the rough cowboys, and how easily she replied to their remarks.

For a moment the old anger surfaced. Jeannie had charmed everyone, flirted with everyone until he'd almost exploded. When he called her on it, she'd act all hurt and upset. It had all been a game to her. One with disastrous consequences. He studied Maggie, annoyed to find her attitude more friendly than flirtatious. Her wide-eyed curiosity about ranch life appealed to the men and they were knocking themselves out to explain everything to her.

Maggie felt Kyle's eyes on her but ignored him. She gave every appearance of listening to what Pete told her about shoeing horses on the range. But her attention split, only one part really listened, the other tried to figure out her reaction to Kyle Carstairs every time he came near her.

It was odd, but she felt attuned to him. She knew when he watched her, could feel the stroke of attention like a touch. She wished she dare turn and meet his gaze, hold it until he looked away first. But she wouldn't give him that satisfaction. An imp of mischief took hold. Maybe she'd have to prove to him that she wasn't interested in him. Maybe playing up to one of the cowboys—

Lance caught her eye, his studying her. He flicked a quick glance to Kyle, back to Maggie, a slow grin starting. Maggie flushed. Had he read her mind? When he winked at her, she looked away. Too bad she didn't feel the same attraction to Lance. He was handsome, tough with the men, yet had a sensitivity about him that she found immensely appealing. However, no attraction simmered between them, not like she felt with—

"If you'd like, you can come with me this afternoon," Lance said easily. "I can show you some more of the ranch."

"She has work to do here," Kyle growled, frowning at his foreman. "I pay her for housework, not to keep you company while you work."

Lance grinned and shrugged. "Sure thing, boss. Thought Maggie might like to see some of the ranch, that's all. You know, have her get to know the place she now calls home."

"She's not going to be here long enough to call this home," Kyle said, glaring at Maggie.

The men stopped eating and stared at Kyle, then Maggie. Slowly, one by one, they looked at each other. Conversation lagged for several minutes, then finally picked up again.

Maggie wanted to throw something. There was no need for him to announce to the entire table that she wasn't wanted.

She raised her eyebrows and started to say something, thought better of it and snapped her mouth closed. If the reports from the agency were to be believed, Kyle was going to have a long wait to find a replacement. And while she didn't plan to stay forever, she wanted to leave on her terms, not his.

She smiled at Lance. "Thanks for the offer. Maybe on my day off." Throwing Kyle a saucy look, she dared him to deny she would have some free time. No matter how hard a boss he proved, everyone got time off.

"I'll take you around on your day off, if you want to see the rest of the ranch," Kyle said, reaching for the coffeepot and refilling his cup.

Maggie thought she'd enjoy seeing the ranch with Lance, but wasn't so sure about going with Kyle. Still, he'd know more about everything. And would share what he wanted her to know, no more. Maybe she could get him to unbend a little before her day off so the day wouldn't be awkward. She wondered if he ever unbent? Did he ever laugh and joke like the other men did? What did he do with his off time?

With lunch over, Maggie returned to cleaning. She had made inroads in the living room and wanted to finish before starting dinner. The room had been neglected for too long. She had dusted everything, cleaned the pictures, and vacuumed the rug, floor and furniture. She wanted to wash the windows so the room would sparkle. There was something very satisfying about bringing order out of chaos. She liked knowing she was making a difference in the room, in the house. To the men.

Kyle had gone into his office to work after lunch, and Maggie heard his voice from time to time, on the phone she supposed. Getting the window cleaner and a roll of paper towels, she began the final task in the room. As she worked, her gaze was drawn time and again to the rich green grass of the range that spread out before her. In the far distance the peaks of Snowy Mountains rose from the high plains. Snowcapped even in summer, they glittered beneath the bright sun. She saw the trees near the house sway in the wind, and smiled. This would be a perfect setting for a romance novel. She could describe the lushness of the ranch. Maybe have her heroine and hero get lost in the vast range. She frowned; that wouldn't work, the hero would know his way around and—

"Maggie?"

She turned. Kyle stood inches away. She hadn't heard him come in.

"Yes."

"What are you doing?"

"Washing windows." What did it look like she was doing?

"You haven't moved a muscle in minutes. I know, I watched you."

She shook her head and turned back to the window. The cleaner had run and dried. Had she been daydreaming again? Guiltily, she sprayed the cleaner on again and wiped hard to eradicate the streaks. "Was there something you wanted?"

"I realized after lunch that we hadn't discussed your days off. I thought the usual ones of Saturday and Sunday."

"What about meals for the men on those days?" she asked. Embarrassment rampant, she tried to work while she talked. She didn't want him to fire her for day-dreaming. Three times before was enough.

"We can get our own."

"I don't mind cooking, if you want. If I can write the rest of the day. I don't have anyplace else to go," she said.

"Most of the men take off for town on Saturdays. You might make something ahead for Sunday dinner that we can heat up."

She nodded, every inch of her body aware of Kyle's proximity. Diligently, she sprayed another pane, began to wipe it clean. Distracted with her reactions around him, she tried to cover her feelings with work.

"What were you doing when I came in?" He refused to let it go.

"I guess I was thinking about the ranch. It's pretty here. You can see the mountains in the distance; between here and there all the range is green with grass. I can just see some cattle on that rise to the left."

"The room looks nice," he said almost grudgingly. He had work to do. He didn't have time to hang around his housekeeper while she washed windows. But he was curiously reluctant to leave. Glancing around, he noticed how tidy she'd made everything; even the pictures on the walls sparkled. She was right, when she worked, she proved to be a hard worker. But he knew she'd been a million miles away when he'd walked into the room.

"The pictures are of your family?" Maggie asked when she turned to see if he had left and found him staring at the photographs.

"My brother and sister. My folks died when we were young."

"I'm sorry. Do your brother and sister live near here?"

"Angel lives in Laramie; she teaches at the university. Rafe and his wife have a spread in Jackson Hole."

"So he's a rancher, like you?"

Kyle turned to face her, his face impassive. "He's always been a rancher. He kept us with him after our folks died, finished raising Angel and me. The Rafter C belongs to all of us, not just me."

"But you run it."

"Yeah, I run it."

"Very successfully, I'd say," Maggie said with a smile.

Kyle's expression hardened. Tension filled the room. "Well enough," he retorted.

Maggie wondered what she'd said wrong. Most people liked being complimented on doing something well. She had been about to congratulate herself on managing a conversation for several minutes without Kyle getting angry. Obviously she'd said something to touch him off, but what?

"Let's get one thing clear up front," he said, glaring down at her. "This is a family ranch. I don't own it all. And I have no intention of sharing it with anyone. Especially someone as flighty as you."

Maggie stared at him. Was he nuts?

"Excuse me, did I miss something in the conversation? I don't want to share this ranch with you. I'm here to work. When I finish my book, I'm going to move back to town and get an apartment of my own and never have to answer to anyone again."

"Right."

She fumed at his sarcastic tone. Boldly she stepped closer and jutted her chin up at him. "Listen to me, Mr. Hot-Shot Rancher, I'm not making a play for you or any other man. I've been clearly told to forget trying to entice anyone. I don't have what it takes, remember? So I'm focused on my new job and my goal to write a novel. I'm certainly not making a play for a bossy, arrogant rancher who can't even keep a housekeeper for longer than a month!''

"He either did a number on you or you're trying to do one on me," Kyle drawled.

"I'm not trying to do anything on you. I'm here to keep house, nothing more."

"And write your book," he added slyly.

"That, too."

"I've seen women use their wiles to try to get their way. I'm not susceptible this time around," he warned.

Outraged, Maggie slammed her fists on her hips and stepped even closer, until she could feel the radiant heat from Kyle's body, until she could smell Kyle's scent.

"Forget it, cowboy. I've had my fill of domineering, bossy, arrogant men. My father was one, my ex-fiancé was one. You would be my last choice, even if I considered such a thing."

"Good, just so we understand each other." He paused a heartbeat, then relaxed a fraction. "I was engaged once myself. To a woman who only wanted the ranch and the perks the money could buy."

She blinked, her anger fleeing instantly. Behind the evenly spoken words, Maggie recognized the hurt and disillusion he'd die if he knew he'd revealed. No wonder he suspected her. His experience with the opposite sex didn't appear to be any better than hers.

"Well, don't paint me with that brush. I don't want your ranch, your money or you." *Liar.* Her conscience whispered how much she would like to know him better. See where the sensual pull that played each time she drew near would lead. Clamping down on those thoughts, she forced herself to keep her glare in place.

Kyle stared at her and wished he could say the same thing. He didn't trust her any farther than he could throw her, but he wanted her. Suddenly every instinct he owned honed in on the slender woman standing so boldly before him. He hadn't felt like this since he'd discovered Jeannie's betrayal. He didn't like it. He wanted his women willing, compliant, and far from the ranch. He had no intentions of getting tangled up with this bit of fluff just to ease an itch. Lust he could control. And there was nothing else between them.

"—with Lance."

"What?"

"I said there's no need to show me the ranch on the weekend, I'll go with Lance."

"Like hell you will. I'm the boss of the spread, and I don't want you and Lance mixing it up. If you need to see the ranch, I'll take you."

"Well, we wouldn't want to think I'm making a play for you, would we?"

She smiled up at him with so much mockery in her look he wanted to wipe her face clean. His hands fisted at his sides and he found it almost impossible to remain where he stood.

"I'd know."

Her smile faltered for a split second, then she upped the wattage. "I'm sure you would, cowboy. You probably have women coming on to you all the time. Gets old, does it?"

"Nothing I can't handle." Slowly he relaxed his hands, stepped closer, his eyes narrowed with intent. She stepped back, alarm flaring. She didn't want to unleash that anger.

"Too late, sugar," Kyle muttered as he reached out and slid his hand beneath the silky hair to the nape of her neck. His mouth came down on hers. Maggie opened hers to shriek a stop, but she was too late, just as he had said. His lips covered hers in a searing kiss.

Scalding heat swept through her, and the muscles in her legs grew weak. Pulsating life pounded, tingling awareness focused on the man holding her head for his kiss. His lips moved against hers in an erotic dance that shimmered through every nerve ending. When his tongue made a brief foray into the dark cavern of her mouth, Maggie moaned softly in unexpected delight.

She was greedy, she admitted. She wanted more. Moving closer, she was shocked when her body came into contact with his. His other arm encircled her and drew her into the tight embrace against his rock-hard length. His chest was solid against her softness, his legs strong enough to support them both. She put her arms around his back, feeling the heat through his shirt, tracing the strong corded muscles.

On fire, burning up from within, Maggie couldn't breathe, couldn't hear anything with the blood pounding wildly through her veins. She could only feel, and wonder. It was as good as the books hinted. Better.

Kyle eased back, his hands on her shoulders now, his eyes hooded and watchful. Maggie slowly lifted her lids and gazed at him, knowing her feelings must show, unable to summon the strength to hide them.

"A scene for your book?" he asked huskily.

Instantly she dropped her hands and turned away, curiously hurt. Had the kiss meant nothing to the man? Had she been the only one to feel anything?

"Maybe," she replied saucily. Damage control, however late, was definitely in order. She raised her head, threw back her shoulders and marched over to the windows to continue cleaning. She hoped passionately that he couldn't see how weak her knees still felt, how her heart hammered in her chest, how the blood still sang with the memory of his touch. She licked her lips and tasted him. Cravings filled her. She wanted more. And knew any more would be dangerous beyond belief.

"I'll apologize if you want," he said gruffly.

"Whatever for? A kiss is nothing. You've made your position clear and I hope I have, too. We have nothing each other wants and I'll stay away from you. You stay away from me." She was proud of her voice. It didn't shake. But, please, God, let him leave.

After several moments of silence, Maggie chanced looking over her shoulder. Kyle had gone.

Slumping down in the nearest chair, she lightly rubbed her lips with her fingertips, reliving every second of their kiss. For someone who didn't like her, he did a credible job of kissing.

Much to her dismay, Maggie wasn't able to toss off the kiss as she wanted. Its memory resurfaced time and time again as she worked during the afternoon. She'd be dusting a table and the next thing she knew she found herself staring off into space, remembering Kyle's touch, remembering how she felt when his lips moved against hers, when his body pressed into hers. It was nothing at all like Don's kisses. And nothing as tame as the ones she'd read about in books. Shaking her head, she'd return to her task, only to find herself thinking more about the kiss than the work she had to do.

Giving up in exasperation, she stormed into the kitchen to prepare the evening meal. Maybe that would take her mind off Kyle Carstairs and his killer kiss.

Stirring a batch of mashed potatoes when Lance sauntered into the kitchen, all cowboy charm, Maggie looked up and smiled. No hidden undertones here. He was a male on the prowl and they both knew it.

"Howdy, darlin'. Need any help?" he asked, leaning against the kitchen counter close to her, watching her.

"You can set the table if you want." It soothed her pride that he flirted with her. At least one man on the ranch wasn't anxious for her to leave.

"Could. Maybe I was just being friendly and wanted to watch you work."

"Get a charge out of watching others work, huh?" She grinned at him. He was nice, friendly. Not like some men she could mention.

"Beats working myself."

"Actually, you could do me a favor, if you wouldn't mind?"

"Anything, darlin'."

Maggie flushed at his flirting. She wasn't used to it and didn't know how to respond. "I haven't had a chance to unload my computer from my car. Maybe you could bring it in for me and set it up?"

"Could." He nodded. "Where are your keys?"

"In my purse, on the dresser in my bedroom. It's the room at the top of the stairs."

"I'll find them."

Moving away, his boots stomping slightly on the wooden floor, Lance went to find her keys.

Maggie put the potatoes back on the stove to keep warm and checked the biscuits. They were perfect, just a minute or two away from being done. She closed the oven door and turned to get the plates and silverware for the table.

She heard the rumble of masculine voices and stopped to listen.

"What the hell are you doing coming from Maggie's room?"

Kyle's voice. Her heart dropped. Tossing everything on the table, she ran out into the hall.

"—keys so I can unload her computer and set it up for her."

"She ask you?"

"As a matter of fact, yes." Lance's eyes danced in amusement as he faced off against Kyle.

Maggie halted when she reached them. A person would have to be dead to miss the tension that filled the hallway. The two men were of a size. They looked ready to fight at the drop of a hat.

"Is there a problem?" She didn't want to be there, but if she was the cause, no matter how unknowing, she thought she should do something to ease the situation.

Kyle shook his head and held out his hand to Lance. "I'll get her computer. There's room in the office. She can use the table near the window."

Lance hesitated a moment, glanced at Maggie and winked. "Fine." He dropped the keys into Kyle's outstretched hand. "Guess I'll be setting the table, after all."

Kyle looked at him sharply. Lance shrugged, grinned, and headed back toward the kitchen. "I offered my services to Maggie. She had a couple of suggestions."

Kyle reached out and snagged Maggie's arm as she turned to follow Lance. She looked up, surprised. Shimmering waves of excitement hit her and she wondered for a foolish moment if he planned to kiss her again.

"Lance is my foreman, not some kitchen help."

"He offered."

"What other services did he offer?" Kyle grit his teeth. He didn't care. He couldn't care. But he also couldn't walk away from her until he knew. What else had Lance offered?

CHAPTER FOUR

BEFORE Kyle could say another word, Maggie whirled around and rushed to the kitchen. She snatched up the hot pad and opened the oven door. The smell of burnt bread filled the kitchen just as the cowboys began to troop in.

One groaned. Maggie turned, her face stricken, holding the large cookie sheet of biscuits. Dumping the sheet on the counter, she flipped one biscuit over; its bottom was scorched. Turning, she glared at Kyle as he followed her into the kitchen.

"This is all your fault, Kyle Carstairs," she said, scraping them off the pan.

"You should have set the timer," he said, coming up behind her. Reaching around her, he scooped up one and examined the black bottom.

"Ha. I was doing fine until you caused me to forget cooking." She began to place biscuit dough on a second cookie sheet. "I was watching them. I had everything under control until you started berating Lance for being in my room."

Instant silence filled the kitchen. Maggie closed her eyes and stifled a groan. Shaking her head, she resumed placing the cut biscuit dough on the cool pan. She'd watch this batch without distraction and make sure it didn't burn. No matter what Kyle got up to, she would concentrate on cooking and not on his arrogant ways.

"Pete, start dishing up. Not that it's the business of any of you, but I went to her room to get her car keys

58

to unload her computer," Lance said, calmly reaching for the platter of ham.

"And then you had to jump to conclusions and make a fuss," she whispered to Kyle, trying to avoid the interest of the men seated around the table.

"What was I to think, seeing a man come from your room?" he whispered in return, his back to the men.

"Think whatever you want, just don't jump to conclusions about me. You'll probably be wrong." She turned and almost bumped into him. Placing her hand on his chest, she pushed. It was like trying to move a mountain.

"You're in my way."

"I knew you'd be a problem."

"I'm not the problem! If you hadn't gotten so upset with Lance over nothing, none of this would have happened," she snapped back.

"While you're here, I'm responsible for you. Think of me as in loco parentis."

"Give me a break! I have no need for a father, thank you very much. I'm old enough to live my own life the way I want. Move!"

Kyle slowly stepped aside and watched as she stormed over to the stove and grabbed the coffee. He scraped the bottoms of the last biscuits and tossed them into the basket, setting it in the center of the table.

He sat at the head and heaped his plate with the ham and mashed potatoes and green beans Maggie had prepared.

There was plenty of food for everyone. Feeling proud of the fact, Maggie took the vacant chair next to Kyle and began to serve herself. No complaints about going hungry this night. It would have been perfect if the biscuits hadn't burned.

She glanced up at the odd expressions on the faces of the men. One by one they took a bite of potatoes, and then looked puzzled. Billy added salt and pepper to his, took another bite. His gaze slid across the table and met hers. Smiling gamely, he cut a hunk of ham.

"What did you do to the potatoes?" Kyle's angry voice interrupted her musing. She looked at him.

"Nothing. They're boxed. I planned on baked potatoes, but forgot to put them—" He didn't need to hear she'd forgotten to put them in the oven in time and had to resort to boxed ones.

"We eat mashed potatoes all the time; they never taste like this."

She scooped up some and sampled. They were sweet! Suddenly she remembered, she had been thinking how her heroine would never be caught in a kitchen in her story. Had she been daydreaming again and picked up sugar instead of salt to season the potatoes? Oh, God, couldn't she get one single meal right?

"They do taste a bit odd. Maybe the drying process altered the taste, or the milk started to go bad." There wasn't enough money in Wyoming to get her to confess before all these men that she had been so stupid to put sugar instead of salt into the mashed potatoes.

Kyle stared at her. Nervously Maggie took a sip of ice tea and prayed he would not attack her in front of everyone. "Shall I make a fresh batch?" she asked just as the buzzer rang for the oven.

Grateful for the respite, she jumped up and withdrew the golden biscuits. Sighing with relief that these turned out perfectly, she gave each man two.

"We'll make it through with these, but maybe next time you should taste them before serving them," Kyle said.

"Good idea." She smiled brightly, more with relief than anything else, and sat back at her place.

"Odd potatoes or not, boss, this beats us cooking," one of the men said.

Kyle had to agree with him, but only by a bit. At least when he or one of the other men cooked they could count on plenty of hot, good food.

As housekeepers went, Maggie was the worst cook he'd seen. But she kept trying, he had to give her that. And she was the easiest on the eyes. In fact she looked downright pretty. He frowned and forced his gaze away. She was too pretty for the ranch. He remembered his mother; she'd been pretty as a child, but looking at her pictures now, he noticed how plain she'd seemed. He remembered more how loving she had always been, how there had been cookies and milk every day, how she'd baked pies and cakes for the men, and because her husband loved sweets. She'd not spent hours every day on her hair or her makeup. And she had been content to work in the home. He never remembered her asking to go into town or out in the evenings. Hadn't her life been complete on the ranch with her family?

Unlike Jeannie. His former fiancée had stayed at the ranch several times, yet always wanted to go into Cheyenne, down to Fort Collins or Denver. She liked parties, nightclubs and dances. And pretty clothes. Clothes totally unsuitable to ranch life.

He flicked a glance to Maggie as she ate quietly. At least Maggie made an effort to dress appropriately. She'd worn tennis shoes today instead of her new boots, but the jeans and cotton shirt were suitable, if a bit snug. But clothes alone didn't make a woman suitable for ranch work.

Not that ranch work was what Miss Maggie Foster wanted, if he could believe her. She considered herself a *writer.* He wondered when she thought she'd find the time to actually sit down and write. Especially if she kept the house up to the standards she set with the living room and kitchen.

"Nice dinner, ma'am, despite the potatoes," Jack said, pushing back his chair.

"And the biscuits. The second batch came out good," Billy said.

Maggie smiled, hoping the heat in her cheeks didn't show. She grew more and more determined to improve her cooking. Breakfast had been perfect, why had she let her mind wander when she cooked dinner?

"I still say it beats me having to cook," Lance added, tilting back in his chair and sipping from the cup of hot coffee. He smiled at Maggie, his eyes studying her.

"It was good," Trevor said as he rose and headed out.

"Mighty fine, ma'am."

"Good night."

One by one the men left the house until only Kyle remained at the table with her. "Had enough?" she asked, preparing to rise to clear the table and do the dishes.

"Of what? Dinner or your attempts to play housekeeper?"

"Dinner," she said, rising. "I'm the best bet you have for housekeeper." She reached for a stack of dirty plates.

"Doesn't say much."

"You're the one who drove the others off."

"Is that what Mrs. Montgomery told you?" he asked, tilting back in his chair, his hands tucked into the front slash pockets of his jeans. He looked totally masculine.

Maggie paused a moment, her eyes feasting on him. Then she resolutely moved to the sink.

"Yes."

"Let's see, when Rachel first left, it took two weeks to get someone. Her name was Alice. She was allergic to hay. I guess since I insisted we keep hay on the ranch for the animals I could be accused of running her off."

Maggie tried not to smile and ran water into the sink.

"And number two?" she asked, intrigued by this un-expected playful side of her austere boss. Especially after a less than perfect meal. Her father would have been ranting and raving for hours at her ineptitude.

"Ah, number two came a week later. Ms. Patricia Dare. Only she dared nothing. She didn't like the iso-lation, didn't like being so far from Cheyenne, didn't like the language of the men, didn't like the wind blowing constantly."

"I didn't notice any bad language," Maggie put in.

"Wait a few days. They're on the best behavior around you. It'll wear off when they're hot and tired and grumpy."

She slid her eyes toward him. "I've seen you that way and not heard anything so bad." Giving up the thought of washing the dishes for a few minutes, she turned off the water and leaned her back against the sink.

He grinned and her heart flopped over. Unable to move her eyes, she could only stare and feel more alive than ever in her life. What was it about Kyle? He had two eyes like everyone else. Well, maybe his were more sexy than a man had a right to have, especially when he narrowed them to gaze down at her. He had a nose and a mouth like everyone else. But unlike anyone else, his mouth had kissed her silly. Her body grew warm with the memory.

"That's because I'm on my best behavior, too. Sugar in the potatoes notwithstanding, having you is better than us fixing our own meals."

"I wouldn't have burned the biscuits if you and Lance hadn't been having words," she said primly. She had hoped he would not mention the potatoes. She should have known better.

"We weren't having words, I simply asked what the hell he was doing in my house coming from your room."

Kyle's grin faded and he looked annoyed. "Next time you need help, ask me."

"I could have managed my computer. It's heavy, but I loaded it into my car. He offered, so I thought I'd take him up on it."

"I'll get it and put it in the office."

"I don't want to be in your way."

"If you do your job right, you won't have time to be in the study during the day. We won't conflict. If I have to work at night, you'll just have to put up with my presence."

Which would probably prove so distracting she would not get a single word written. She knew her imagination would fly if Kyle were nearby, but in the right direction? Somehow she kept seeing herself as the heroine to his hero. And that was never going to happen.

"Thank you, then. It will be more convenient than in my room."

"I'll get it now."

As Maggie did the dishes, she thought about their conversation. Maybe Mrs. Montgomery had stretched the truth a bit. Kyle hadn't proved impossible yet. He'd certainly told her off a couple of times, but he had the right of it each time. And he hadn't said much about dinner's disaster. He'd given her more chances than the other places of employment had, and that was definitely in his favor. She wished he had continued telling her about the other housekeepers. If the first two left for the reasons he'd given, it didn't make him a demanding boss at all. Why had the others left so soon after arriving?

Too tired to be creative by the time Maggie had her computer hooked up, she loaded the chapters she'd already written and worked on them. She didn't know where Kyle had gone, and refused to admit to being disappointed he didn't have work in the study that night.

Starting at chapter one, gradually she found herself dissatisfied with the descriptions; they didn't really capture the essence of what she wanted for her hero. Maybe she could study Kyle more closely and get a better feel of how to describe him on paper.

The words began to blur. She had to get to sleep if she was to get up early enough to prepare breakfast. With a sigh, she turned off the machine wondering where Kyle was and how he spent his evenings.

Maggie felt as if her head had barely touched the pillow when loud, rapid knocking on her door woke her from a deep sleep. Sitting upright in surprise, she realized dawn was still a half hour away.

"Maggie, dammit, wake up!" Kyle pounded on her door and called her name. Was there a fire?

She scrambled from the bed and ran to the door, flinging it open. Blinking in the bright hall light, she peered up at him.

"What's wrong?"

He slowly lowered his still-raised hand as he took in her appearance. Her hair, tousled and disheveled from sleeping, swirled around her face like a soft brown cloud. A sleep crease from her sheet slashed across her cheek. Her eyes were half closed against the light. And she wore a pale blue, skimpy satiny sleep shirt that draped over her, hugging her curves and valleys.

Kyle felt a burst of desire unexpected and hard. He stepped closer, skimming the back of his fingers down her flushed, warm cheek.

"Is there a fire?" she asked, shaking her head to come awake.

"No fire." He rested his hands on her shoulders, drawing her closer as his gaze traveled down to her pink polished toes. Her legs were bare, tanned, shapely. The sleep shirt, stopping at the midpoint of her thighs, almost fell off one shoulder.

"Kyle?" Maggie took in his attire. He wore only a terry robe. At least she thought that was all he wore. She could see his bronzed chest in the deep vee of the short robe; his muscular legs were bare.

He drew her up against him, slowly, as if allowing her plenty of time to resist, to deny him what he wanted. Maggie moved as if in a trance. Had he wakened to seek her out? Why was he there?

His lips covered hers and he moved them until she opened her mouth. At the first foray of his tongue, she slipped her hands up to his shoulders, to his neck, to thread themselves in his thick hair. His face was clean shaven and soft, his hair still damp from his shower. Not that Maggie consciously noticed. She had enough trouble breathing, enough trouble keeping her legs beneath her.

But somewhere it registered that he had already had his shower and probably wore nothing beneath his robe. As she wore nothing beneath her shirt.

"Maggie." He pulled back, breathing hard.

"Mmm?" She wanted to step back into his embrace, let their kiss go on and on until—

"Where are my clothes?"

"What?" She snapped open her eyes and stared at him. "What do you mean, where are your clothes? In your—ohmygod!" Whirling, she raced down the stairs and into the kitchen, flicking on the lights as she made her way through the house, heading for the laundry room. Ohmygod, she breathed, flinging up the lid to the washer. There in damp array sat his jeans and dark shirts. She had forgotten to put them in the dryer yesterday! On the floor before the washer sat two more loads of clothes, all waiting to be washed.

"Damn!" Kyle had followed her and stood in the doorway, his gaze immediately recognizing the situation.

"I can dry them right away." She pulled the heavy damp denims from the washer and stuffed them into the dryer.

"Denim takes forever to dry."

"Nonsense, they'll be dry by the time you finish breakfast," she said, crossing her fingers as she hit the On button. Putting soap into the washer, she scooped up another load and started that, as well.

"If you think I'm going to breakfast dressed like this, you're crazy," he said.

She looked at him, and her heart melted. Her knees grew weak again and she held on to the washer like a lifeline. He looked like he just got up from bed. His hair was mussed, from her own hands. His eyes glittered at her and in the uncertain light it looked like he wanted her. Which just proved her imagination worked even first thing in the morning. Don had assured her no man would want her; why would someone like Kyle ever look at her that way?

She pushed away.

"I'm sorry. I guess I was so caught up in cleaning, I forgot to change the loads. I'll make sure they are all done today."

"Can you keep your mind on it?" he asked harshly.

"Yes." He had a right to be angry. It took less than twenty seconds to load the dryer and push the button; why hadn't she remembered? Maybe the kiss had had something to do with forgetting everything. It would have been so easy even if she'd put the clothes in to dry before going to bed. She should have remembered!

"You'll excuse me for wondering. How could you forget something so simple?"

"I just did, okay? It won't happen again."

"I'm putting my money on that it will happen again. Maggie, you're one strange woman. You go off into your own little world so far the house could burn down around you and I don't think you'd notice."

"So this housekeeper might be the one that just wandered away in her mind?" she joked, trying to ease the tension that shimmered between them.

"No, sweetheart, this one might be the one I fire," he said slowly.

"Please don't, Kyle. I'll do better, I promise. It's just my way of coping."

"Coping with what?"

"My dad. He . . . nothing I did ever pleased him. He wanted me to be like my mother and I never could. She left him when I was little. Left us both. He's such a hard taskmaster, expects perfection. So I'd imagine I did things his way. That he liked what I did." Loved me, she wanted to say, but stopped short before revealing that.

"And imagined a lot of other things to make life more bearable?" he asked.

She nodded. "But things are different here. I'm doing a good job. I know I've messed up a little—"

He laughed. "You've messed up more than anyone I've ever known. I'd hate to see your definition of messing up a lot!"

"But I'm getting better. I know now to fix tons of food. I won't put sugar in the potatoes again. I'll use the timer so I don't burn things. I've already cleaned the living room and hall. And I'll finish up the rest of the house before you know it."

"You can stay. But just temporarily, Maggie. I told you that from the first, so don't get settled in too much."

"I know." Once she sold her book, it wouldn't matter. She could live wherever she wanted. And write full time.

Still, it hurt just a little that he kept reminding her she was here temporarily.

"I'll be in the study; bring breakfast there," he said. Glancing down the length of her, he met her eyes. "And I suggest you change before starting breakfast or you'll have ten cowboys over you like flies on honey."

"Only ten?" she asked provocatively. Was he immune to her? Even after kissing her? Or was it because he'd kissed her and found her lacking?

He reached out and rubbed the pad of his thumb gently over her lower lip. "I think Jack's immune, too old."

She trembled at his touch, at his words. He'd included himself in the group of cowboys. It warmed her heart like nothing ever had.

"What a kind man you are," she said.

"Kind?"

"To say such a nice thing. I've never had anyone hint I could be desirable."

Kyle groaned and pulled her into his arms. "What do you think these kisses have been about?" he asked as his mouth closed over hers again.

She drove him crazy. As provocative as hell and she didn't even have the slightest clue. As innocent as a babe, which enchanted him, and confused him. He liked women experienced, who knew the score, and were not interested in commitment. He didn't want to feel anything for her. He wanted her gone.

But not just yet. His tongue tasted her sweetness, his chest savored the feel of her soft breasts pressed against him. His arms cherished the rounded body that so trustingly leaned into him. If he weren't careful, he'd want more from her than anyone had ever given, including Jeannie.

At the thought of his former fiancée, Kyle's ardor dimmed. He ended the kiss, raised his head. Maggie opened her eyes and stared up at him, the wonder clearly evident. He felt ten feet tall, and wary as hell.

"Change your clothes," he said. Releasing her, he tightened the belt on his robe and headed for the study. He wasn't about to fall for some starry-eyed optimist who was looking for kindness. He had his priorities, the ranch first and everything else a distant second. Time he called the employment agency again and hurry them up on the replacement housekeeper.

Maggie prepared breakfast in a daze. She couldn't believe Kyle had kissed her this morning, twice. She didn't understand why. While she found his kisses wonderful, she knew her own were woefully inadequate. Hadn't Don told her that several times? Maybe it was because Kyle hadn't been around other women in a long time. Maybe being the only woman available for kisses, he made do.

Wow, if that was making do, she'd love to see all-out seduction. On the other hand, she probably couldn't handle it. Already she felt as if she were in over her head. She hated to disappoint him, but she'd reached the limit of her experience. She hadn't a clue how to progress. Even if he wanted to progress. And by the way he pulled away, she doubted it.

By midmorning Maggie had a grocery list that didn't end. Knowing how much time it had taken her to shop the last time, she knew she had better get going in order to buy everything, put it away and have time to prepare the evening meal. Making a huge stack of sandwiches, she wrapped them and left them in the refrigerator, with a note in the center of the table telling the men where to find the food.

She headed for the yard, wondering who would teach her how to drive one of the pickup trucks, or if she needed anyone to show her how. Kyle had said he would, but she didn't want to be confined in the cab of a truck with him. Her mind kicked into overdrive anytime she came near him. How could she concentrate on driving techniques if she wondered every second whether he'd kiss her again?

The only truck available was the big blue and white one nosed up against the barn. She crossed the yard and opened the door. The key jutted in the ignition. Climbing up into the cab, she slammed the door and took stock. How hard would it be? A bit different from a car, he'd said. But everything looked the same. She adjusted the seat. Kyle or Lance must have driven it last, the seat was so far back. Fiddling with the mirror, she took a deep breath and started the engine.

No one came to see who had started the truck. In fact, she hadn't seen hide nor hair of anyone since Kyle passed through the house sometime after breakfast, fully dressed in his dry clothes. Which reminded her, she hadn't put that second washload in the dryer. Slowly she reversed the truck until she stopped by the back door. Putting it into park, she dashed inside to throw the clothes in the dryer, start the last washload.

In only moments she turned onto the highway that led to Cheyenne, pleased she had managed on her own, and forgotten nothing. Her confidence soared.

By the end of the week, Maggie felt much more secure in her position. She had mastered shopping, meal planning, and even cooking. Only once during the week had she burned anything, and she had hidden the evidence before the men discovered it.

The house shone. She'd cleaned everything from top to bottom, including Kyle's bedroom. Laundry still proved a challenge to her, to remember to put wet clothes in the dryer, but she made it a habit to wander into the laundry room just after mealtime.

But her book had suffered. Too tired at night to do anything but fall into her bed, she had not touched a chapter since that first night. Determined to get busy on the novel, she hurried through her chores Friday morning, giving the house a lick and a promise. Since everything had been cleaned in the last couple of days, there was little to do. She made a stew, set it on the stove to simmer slowly, and wiped up after lunch.

The afternoon loomed free, and she planned to take full advantage of it.

For the first time since she arrived, she wanted to go outside and discover what she could about the ranch. Changing into her boots, she brushed her hair back into a ponytail, to keep the hair from her face in the afternoon's breeze.

Strolling to the barn, Maggie avidly took in everything her eye spotted. The horses in the corral dozed in the early afternoon sun, one back leg bent, resting on the tip of a hoof, heads lowered, eyes closed.

The blue and white pickup she'd driven to the store was parked nose into the gray barn. She smiled as she remembered how proud she'd felt the other day when she reached home without mishap. And the long assessing look Kyle had given her when he found out she'd taken the truck and done enough shopping to last a couple of weeks.

The wide double doors of the barn stood open and the cavernous interior looked dark and mysterious compared to the bright sunshine. The scent of hay and horses mingled in the breeze. It was hushed, no voices murmured in the background. Most of the men were on the range. Doing tallies, she remembered. Only four had been in for lunch.

She paused in the doorway to let her eyes adjust to the dimmer light. The hayloft ran the length of the barn on both sides, open in the middle. Bales of hay stacked up five high lined the walls. Loose hay drifted over the edge when the breeze gusted. The stalls were empty. The door to the tack room stood open and Maggie headed for it.

Jack leaned back in a chair, rubbing saddle soap into a set of reins. He glanced up when she stepped inside.

"Hi. I'm taking a walk," Maggie said brightly.

"Howdy. Set a spell. Finally wanting out of the house?"

"Yes. I've caught up on all the work that needs doing right away. Thought I'd find out more about the ranch."

"Any questions, ask away."

Maggie glanced around. Jack had the only chair, and she wouldn't ask him to give it up. She took a blanket from a hook on the wall and folded it on the floor, sinking down so she could watch Jack work as he talked.

A million questions bubbled up. Some from her own curiosity, others slanted to the new idea she had for her book. Jack answered them all patiently, expanding when she requested, explaining terms to her, making sense at last to some of the conversations she'd heard at dinner.

When a horse rode into the yard, Maggie wondered if it might be Kyle. She hadn't seen him since breakfast. He'd been one of the men out doing tallies, so he hadn't come in for lunch. Her hands grew damp with nerves when she thought it might be him. He had maintained his distance since that morning he'd kissed her in the laundry room. But he had not had cause to get angry with her since then. She'd done her job well, and though he watched her during mealtime, he had found no fault. While she was pleased she was beginning to measure up, she lived in hope he'd kiss her one more time before she left.

CHAPTER FIVE

LANCE appeared in the doorway.

"Wondered who you were talking to," he said to Jack, then smiled at Maggie, one finger tipping back his hat.

"Just answering some questions the little lady had. Her first time on a ranch, you know," Jack said.

"Come with me, I'll give you some pointers," Lance invited.

Maggie scrambled up and rehung the blanket. "Thank you, Jack. Hope I didn't drive you crazy with all my questions."

"No, pleasure to talk about ranching. So many people aren't interested in hearing an old man ramble on."

"You didn't ramble, and I found it all fascinating," she said with a sunny smile. Following Lance into the barn, she walked beside him as he led his horse to the rear. Fastening it in cross ties, he began to unsaddle his mount.

"Where did you go today?" she asked, taking careful note of how he did everything. The horse seemed large, but didn't bother Lance. He easily hefted the heavy saddle, dropping it on a stand nearby and turning to grin at Maggie.

"Out to one of the areas where we've got a lot of cattle. We're taking a tally of how many are on that particular bit of range, checking to make sure we've lost none, or none are down and hurting. Or missing."

"Do you do that kind of thing a lot?"

"Enough to insure the well-being of the herd."

"The Rafter C seems to be a very prosperous ranch," she commented.

"Very. One of the top ranches in this part of the country. When Rafe ran the place, he got written up in a journal as a rancher to watch."

"How long ago was that?"

"A few years now. Before I came here. Rafe didn't want a foreman, did all that kind of work himself."

"And where was Kyle?"

"At the university. When he graduated, he started working here as foreman, I guess you'd say."

"Then Rafe left and Kyle took over?"

"Yep. Once their sister graduated from the university, Rafe took off to ride the rodeo circuit. Kyle hired me a few months later."

"And the ranch continues to be very prosperous," she finished, feeling a certain curious pride in the work Kyle had done. His brother might have started things in the right direction, but it was Kyle's work now that kept it prosperous.

"Very prosperous, but why do you care? Worried about your salary?" Kyle's voice sounded behind her.

Maggie turned, startled to find him standing so close to her. She hadn't heard him come in. She saw his horse standing beyond the open doors. How much had he heard? And what interpretations did he put on her questions? Obviously the wrong ones.

"I wasn't *worried* about anything, just curious," she said, flustered. His hat pulled low, his jeans were tight and dusty. Maggie's heart fluttered and she longed to sit somewhere and stare at him until she had her fill. But ever conscious of Lance, and Kyle's unfriendly stare, she looked away.

"Now I wonder why?" Kyle glanced at Lance, back to Maggie. "What are you doing out here?"

"I'm caught up on the housework and wanted to get out for some fresh air," she said pertly, her eyes meeting his, her gaze challenging.

"In the barn?" His tone disbelieving.

"Maggie wanted to know more about the ranch. Jack answered some of her questions. I was going to show her around some," Lance said easily, his gaze meeting Kyle's, his stance loose and at ease.

Ignoring his foreman, Kyle stared at Maggie, his eyes narrowed. "I told you I'd answer any questions you had."

"You weren't here. Lance and Jack were."

"I'm here now."

"I don't mind, boss," Lance interjected.

"Don't you have work to do?" Kyle asked, transferring his gaze to Lance.

"Just report in the findings from the tally. I can do it orally if you like."

"No, write it up. And when the others come in, write up their tallies, too. And while you're waiting, you can unsaddle my horse." Kyle nodded toward the standing horse before stepping closer to Maggie. Taking her arm in his hand, he tugged her toward the large double doors.

Lance hesitated a moment, then shrugged and smiled. "Sure thing, boss."

Kyle marched Maggie out into the yard. In the distance he could see two more men riding in. He kept hold of her arm and moved away from the barn, toward the house.

"Don't you have dinner to fix?" he asked.

"We're having stew and it's simmering now." She tried to release her arm from his grasp, but he ignored her. She didn't like feeling like a recalcitrant child who had to be marched into the house.

"I told you to stay away from the men," Kyle said in a low growl.

"I wasn't doing anything wrong, just asking some questions."

"For your book?"

"Maybe some of the questions. But the rest were because I'm curious."

"Why?" He stopped well back before the back stoop.

"Why not? I live here now, and have never lived on a ranch before. I want to find out more about it."

"Then ask me, as I told you."

"You didn't tell me I couldn't ask questions about the ranch. You just said stay away from your cowboys if I wanted to do research for my book."

He turned and started walking around the house until they reached the front porch. Before them the green grass waved gently in the afternoon breeze, the trees that shaded portions of the house rustled softly. The air was clean and fresh and only the faintest trace of hay and horse could be discerned.

Kyle released her arm and sank down in one of the rockers that lined the wooden porch. Gingerly, Maggie sat in the one next to his.

"Questions?" he said.

"Jack answered a lot I had," she replied.

"He's all right. Stay away from Lance."

"Why?"

"He watches you. He's interested in you. I don't want my foreman's mind on anything but his job."

"How feudal. He's entitled to a life aside from being your foreman."

"Not with some temporary woman more interested in writing about romance than—"

"Than?" she asked, her eyes narrowed as she suspected the ending of his thought.

"Than in doing chores around here."

"That isn't what you started to say, is it?"

He took his hat off and dropped it on the wooden floor beside his chair. Raking his fingers through his hair, he leaned against the high back of the rocker and watched her from lowered lids.

"That's what I said. Never mind what I started to say."

"I have a good imagination."

"I'm beginning to believe it."

Maggie remained silent.

"Is it all made up? Your book, I mean?" he asked.

"Mostly." She glanced away, studied the cotton-woods that rustled in the breeze. The sound should be soothing; why couldn't she relax?

"Not from first-hand experience?"

"I don't have much experience," she said, her eyes now fixed on the distant horizon. Did she have to spell it out for him? Surely he noticed from her kisses.

"You were engaged."

"What does that have to do with anything?"

"I don't know. Tell me about the engagement."

She shrugged, settled back in her rocker and pushed it to and fro. "I don't see how that has anything to do with my job here."

"It doesn't. Tell me about your engagement."

She flicked a glance and met his heated gaze. "There's not much to tell. My father introduced me to Don. We dated. I thought him very romantic at first. He took me to fancy restaurants, ordered for me, we went dancing. He bought me nice gifts. It was all quite elegant. When he asked me to marry him, I thought it would be perfect, so I said yes."

"Of course, a woman likes presents, likes to be wined and dined. Did you ever give a thought to the years you two would live together? To building a life together?"

"I thought I did. I thought I was in love, now I think I was just infatuated with him. Disenchantment didn't take long. But it took a lot for me to break it off." More than she had thought herself capable of at the time. But it had been the right decision. Marriage between them would have been a monumental mistake. And she had grown up a bit more ending the engagement.

"Why?"

She looked at him. "He has everything a woman would want. He's rich, well-established in his career, has a beautiful home, decorated by a professional. He likes to go out to dinner, dancing, parties."

"He sounds a perfect paragon. I'm surprised you didn't snap him up."

"The more I got to know him, the more like my father he became. I spent the first twenty-one years of my life trying to please a man who could not be pleased. As long as I did exactly what he said, we had a peaceful coexistence. Don was the same. When I dutifully did whatever he requested, our relationship went smoothly. If I refused anything, he got very annoyed."

"What did you refuse?"

She looked at her hands, locked together, fingers tightly binding each other. It really wasn't Kyle's business. None of her life had any impact on his. Why did he even bother to ask? Yet as she hesitated, he prodded.

"Maggie, what did you refuse that made him so annoyed?"

"To sleep with him, for one thing. To try to have a career of my own for another."

He sat up and stared at her, his eyes wide with astonishment. "You were engaged to be married and you never slept with the guy?"

She shook her head. Flicking him a rueful look, she said, "I guess by your surprise that you did sleep with your fiancée."

"Yes. We were to be married." As if that explained it all.

"Oh." She looked away, not surprised. And a little bit envious. She was the anomaly these days. Most people planning to marry had no hesitations about anticipating wedding vows. She did, however. And since she was no longer planning to marry Don, she was glad she had.

"So how do you write romance novels if you have no first-hand experience?" he asked.

"I told you, I have a good imagination."

Kyle reached over and caught her hand in his, threading his fingers between hers. Maggie looked at their linked hands. The heat from his hard palm swept through her like a range fire. The shimmering awareness of his gender flooded her. Her own sense of femininity grew and her body began to clamor for more attention. She drew in a shaky breath and slowly tightened her hold on his hand, her gaze slowly, reluctantly, drawn to his.

"Sometimes there's no substitution for experience," Kyle murmured.

"Are you offering to be the man to give me some?" she asked saucily. Her heart pounded at the thought. If the simple holding of hands almost had her climbing into his lap, what would a full attack on her senses do? She could imagine— She could imagine only so much. She never imagined a simple clasping of hands could so disrupt her equilibrium. So how could she imagine the myriad pleasures making love would bring?

"I can give you some. But strictly as research."

She smiled at his nonsense. "What else but research?"

"I don't want you getting the wrong idea. I have no intention of marrying you."

"Marriage? Why bring that up?"

"You were checking out the financial strength of the ranch with Lance. Trying to determine if it was worth your while?"

She yanked on her hand. Insulted, she no longer wanted to hold hands. Kyle tightened his grip, refusing to release her.

"I wasn't trying to find out how rich you are. For heaven's sake, if I wanted a rich husband, I could have married Don. I don't want any husband. I'm tired of men telling me what to do. I want a chance to do things on my own. See if I can make a life for myself. The last thing I want is to tie myself down with some bossy man who thinks he's God's gift to women."

"So there's no problem, then."

"What do you mean?"

"I'll provide you with the experience you need for your book, and we will both walk away at the end of your stay with no expectations on either side."

She stared at him, her heart caught in her throat. For a long moment she considered his suggestion. Could she do it? Could she allow kisses and caresses and write down the feelings to add authenticity to her writing? And then walk away when the book sold?

She hadn't liked Don's kisses. Didn't miss the man at all. But Kyle's kisses were as unlike Don's as night to day. She felt different when his lips touched hers, when his body pressed against hers. Licking her lips, she could almost taste Kyle on them, just from memory of the last kiss. She wanted more. Yet she was afraid. It was like playing with fire. Could she do it and not get burned?

Kyle watched the expressions chase across her face and almost smiled. She considered every aspect, he could tell. But he had no idea of the outcome. Would she want to explore the sizzling sensuality between them? Or opt to remain safe and chaste? His palm burned where they touched. He longed to draw her into his lap and kiss her until neither could remember their names. His body wanted hers. His control wore thin around her, and he didn't like it. Maybe a few kisses would purge his system of the need that grew stronger each day.

Tugging experimentally, Maggie wasn't sure whether to be relieved or disappointed when he released her hand. She swallowed hard and faced him. Taking in the golden hair in disarray since his fingers had plowed through it, the sun-bronzed skin taut across high cheekbones, the firm lips that had already kissed her senseless, and the strong jaw that reminded her of his strength, she met his gray eyes. "Could I think about it?"

"Sure." He reached for his hat and rose. Leaning over her, he caught her chin between his thumb and fore-tinger. "The offer stays open as long as you want to take to decide. But the offer is with me. Stay away from my men."

"I know." Her breath caught. He was so close he had only to lean over a few more inches and his mouth would touch hers, his lips could bring her the same heady delight she'd felt in the laundry room days ago. Parting her lips slightly to let the breath escape, Maggie leaned forward just a little bit, to bring Kyle even closer—

He straightened and rammed his hat on his head. "See you at dinner." Sauntering off, around the side of the house, he left her stunned, and alone.

Maggie sank back in the rocker in embarrassment. She had practically offered herself to him and he'd walked away. Was it because she hadn't yet said yes to his proposition? Had he seen how much she wanted his kiss? She hoped not. Even if she did take him up on his offer, she wanted to stand up on her own feet, not grow to depend on another man.

She rose and tried the front door. It was unlocked, so she entered the house and headed for her room. Changing from her boots to more comfortable tennis shoes, she headed for the kitchen. Time to do the cornbread and set the table. It was getting close to dinnertime. She'd think about his offer after dinner.

Maggie had prepared the cornbread batter and begun to pour it into the pans when the phone rang. She jumped. It rang so infrequently, it startled her. She waited a moment, but when it rang again, she reached for the extension.

"Hello?"

"Hi, is Kyle there?" a cheery feminine voice asked.

"Hold on." Maggie's curiosity raged. Who was calling Kyle? What woman called him?

She opened the back door preparing to run to the barn to see if he was there when she saw him leaning against the corral fence watching one of the men working a horse.

"Kyle, phone."

He acknowledged her call with a wave and headed for the house.

Maggie resumed her work as he picked up the receiver.

"Hello? Hi, Gillian, what's up?"

Maggie carefully placed the pans in the hot oven, conscious of listening to his side of the call. He couldn't expect privacy if he were in the kitchen with her. If he had wanted to be alone he could have taken it in the office.

"Damn! No, no, it's fine. I'm running late. I just got in. It'll take me a half hour or so to shower and dress. I'll be there before eight."

Maggie carefully checked the stew pots, stirring them gently, every cell in her body focused on Kyle's conversation. Who was Gillian, and where was he going to be by eight?

Kyle replaced the phone and turned to Maggie. He knew she'd heard every word. "I won't be here for dinner."

"I won't set a place," she replied, her eyes on the stew she stirred. *Where are you going? And who with?* she screamed inside. She hoped her expression didn't give away her raging curiosity. And the unexplained hurt. He was obviously going out with Gillian, whoever she was. Her active imagination immediately envisioned a young sexy woman with long red hair, bright green eyes, and a figure to die for. She would be scintillating, and provocative. And enchant Kyle all evening.

Dammit, hadn't he just propositioned her? All but asked her to have an affair with him? Now he was going out with some other woman?

She looked up to tell him she'd decided to decline his offer, but he was gone. Sure, he had to hurry and shower to leave in time to pick Gillian up by eight. He had no time to stand around waiting for her answer.

When the men came in for dinner, Billy asked right away where the boss was. He'd noticed there'd been no place set for Kyle.

"Going out," Maggie said, proud her voice sounded almost normal, that she hadn't growled out the words with all the anger simmering inside. She sat at her usual place, extremely aware of the vacant chair beside her.

Kyle came into the kitchen, dressed in casual slacks, a cream-colored shirt and sports jacket. He looked wonderful. But after one quick glance, Maggie looked away and refused to look at him again. The dull ache in her breast was not because he was dating another woman. She wouldn't let it be.

"Wowee, boss, you sure are duded up. Hot date?" Billy asked, teasing.

Kyle's face darkened. "A friend of mine asked me to escort her to a party," Kyle said shortly.

"Have a good time, Kyle," Jack said.

"Yeah, I'm going to town after dinner myself. It's Friday night and I've worked hard all week," Billy said.

"You go in when you haven't worked hard," Lance murmured.

Billy beamed a smile around the table. "Right. It's party night, right, boss?"

Maggie felt Kyle's gaze on her, but she kept her eyes on her plate. The stew had turned out good, and she tried to be pleased about it. But she was disappointed Kyle wasn't eating it. He only saw her less than successful attempts.

"I won't be late," Kyle said.

"Does that mean tonight or tomorrow morning?" Billy asked irrepressively, his spirits high.

"Billy." Lance's voice held a warning the younger man couldn't ignore. He shut up.

"Take it easy, Kyle. And don't worry about a thing," Lance said, his eyes on Maggie. "I'll take care of things here."

She looked up and met his gaze. Hearing the screen door slam shut, she knew Kyle had gone. Lance smiled easily. And Maggie felt marginally better.

"Want to go into town with me for a few drinks and dancing at a country-western bar?" Lance asked.

She nodded. She sure as shooting didn't want to stay home alone and let her imagination run riot thinking about Kyle and the beautiful Gillian. Ignoring Kyle's warnings to stay away from his men, and especially Lance, she smiled gratefully. "I'd like that. But I'm not sure how good I'll be at the dancing."

"Good enough, I'm sure." He winked and resumed eating.

The conversation around the table turned to the plans of the others. Many of the others were going into town. Jack and Trevor had plans for a television show.

Jack offered to do the dishes, which Maggie gratefully accepted. Before long Lance and Maggie were heading for town. Determined to enjoy herself, and make the evening pleasant for Lance, she hid the hurt Kyle's date had inflicted, and set out to entertain. Lance laughed at the spots in her stories she wanted him to, and asked enough questions to have her expound on everything. The ride to Cheyenne flew by and before Maggie realized it, they were walking into The Last Roundup.

Obviously popular by the friendly greetings called out, Lance waved and called greetings in return. He spotted some friends at a large table and in no time had Maggie seated and introduced. Relieved to see the other women dressed in jeans and shirts as she was, she relaxed and soon was in the middle of the conversation.

It was a wonderful evening. The men took turns dancing with the women, not letting them sit out any sets. The women were friendly and Maggie felt she could develop a strong friendship with one or two. If she were staying, that is.

When she mentioned she was trying to write a romance novel, heads turned and the questions and suggestions came fast and furiously. Everyone had a story of their most romantic moment. Some wanted to know what her story was about, others had ideas they wanted to write about one day.

At one point Maggie laughed and waved her hands. "You have to slow down. I can't hear everyone at once. I wish I had paper and pencil to write down some of these ideas, they're great."

"We'll each write them down and send them to you. Where do you live?"

"The Rafter C. I'm the housekeeper there."

"Of course, she came with Lance."

"Didn't know housekeepers came so pretty. The one my dad had was old and crotchety," one cowboy called out, winking at Maggie.

She smiled and basked in the warm friendliness of the group. They were supportive of her dreams and ambitions, not derogatory. They were friendly and helpful and fun to be with. It was so different from what she was used to, she wanted to stay forever.

But the evening ended all too soon when the band played the last song. Lance said they had to get back. With promises to meet again ringing in her ears, Maggie reluctantly climbed back into Lance's truck and settled down for the long drive home. She was smiling, humming the last song. The evening had been fun.

He played country music softly on the radio and conversation between them was desultory. When he turned onto the blacktop drive that led to the house, Maggie turned to him.

"I had a wonderful evening, Lance. Thank you for inviting me."

"I'm glad you came. Think you can use any of the suggestions from tonight?"

She smiled, remembering. "Maybe one or two. I couldn't believe some of the comments, they were so outrageous. And yet others were so basic, like a simple bouquet of flowers, or a home-cooked meal. It was interesting to see what different people found romantic."

"What do you find romantic, Maggie?"

She shook her head. "Different things. Flowers are nice."

When he pulled into the yard a light shone in the kitchen, but the bunkhouse sat in darkness. The night sky blazed with millions of stars, the moon a mere crescent low on the horizon. He killed the engine and sat back.

"What else, Maggie?"

"I don't know. In my story I have plans for the heroine to give small gifts to the hero. He's not used to getting gifts and thinks that is pretty special."

"And do you—"

The passenger door snapped open, the overhead light flooding the cab of the truck.

"Where the hell have you been?" Kyle was blazing mad. He leaned into the cab and nailed Lance. "Do you have any idea how late it is?"

"After two," Lance replied easily, a smile playing around his lips as he leaned against his door and studied his boss.

"If you wanted to go out, you could have told me!" Kyle said to Maggie, reaching in to unfasten her seat belt.

"What I want or don't want to do on my hours off is none of your business," she said, slapping his hands away and letting the belt slide free. When he reached for her arm, she slapped at him again. "Don't touch me!"

She turned to Lance, annoyed to find his amusement so blatant. "Thank you again."

"Good night, Maggie. Sleep well." He trailed a finger down her cheek.

Kyle stood by her door, ramrod straight, the anger roiling off him in waves. Maggie avoided touching him as she walked to the house, her head held high. He walked beside her like a guard.

"Where were the two of you?" he growled.

"Out," she replied, marching up the steps and into the kitchen. Not pausing a beat, she continued toward the stairs and her room.

He pulled her around and gripped her shoulders. "I asked you a question, you answer it!"

"We went to The Last Roundup. Where I met a lot of nice people and had a grand time." She almost shouted. He wasn't the only one to get angry. Who did he think he was? Her father? "Not that it's any of your business. I didn't ask about your date."

"It wasn't a date. Was that what you and Lance had, a date?"

"Define date. If you pick up some woman and take her to a party, then bring her home, isn't that a date?"

"I told you to stay away from Lance!"

"What, stay home like a dutiful daughter while you're out carousing? I think not."

He exhaled deeply. "Is that what this is about? You're jealous of me taking Gillian to that party? She asked me to go with her several weeks ago. Long before I even met you."

She shrugged from beneath his hands and started for the stairs. "I don't need any explanations. Your life is yours to lead as you wish. As is mine."

"While you work for me you will do as you're told. Stay away from Lance and the other men on this ranch."

"Or?" She turned and glared at him.

"Or you're fired."

She held his gaze, seeing the implacable determination in it. So mad she wanted to burst, Maggie took a deep breath. She would not lose her job over a man who meant nothing to her beyond friendship, yet she refused to let Kyle run roughshod over her like this. It reminded her too much of her father. She was her own person and would fight to retain that.

"Who died and left you king?" she said between clenched teeth. "I'll see whomever I wish on my free time. Where do you come off dictating my love life to me? Do you do that with everyone on the ranch? It's a wonder you can keep anyone."

He ran his hands through his hair and the anger seemed to dissipate. He lowered his hands and stared at her. "You're right. I apologize. It is none of my business. You'd think I'd learn."

Dumbfounded, Maggie's own anger evaporated. Was this a trick? "What do you mean?"

He turned and walked slowly across the kitchen to close the back door. "What you do with your life is your affair. I have no right to tell you to stay away from Lance on your off time. I tried that once before, told my brother-in-law to stay away from my sister. She found that hard to forgive. Think I'd learn a lesson from that. You can see whomever you wish, of course, as long as it doesn't interfere with your work or his." His back still turned toward her, he fiddled with the key in the door.

Knowing they never locked the place, Maggie recognized a stalling tactic when she saw one.

"Go to bed, Maggie."

She didn't want to leave. Something blossomed in her heart as she watched him fiddle with the door, unwilling to turn and face her. And she remembered his offer on the porch.

"Aren't you going to kiss me good-night?"

He whirled, his eyes blazing.

"So you thought about my offer?"

She nodded.

"And?"

"I'm still not sure."

"Then we'll wait on any kisses until you are."

She licked her lips. "I never thought I'd have an affair," she said slowly.

"We'll only go as far as you want." He wasn't much on affairs, either, but he knew where trusting a woman could lead. He was not open for long-term commitment. But for a few days, a few weeks...

She nodded, her skin feeling too tight for her body. He looked at her and she almost flung herself against him to assuage the longings that rose so fiercely. She wanted to feel his kisses, to feel the length of his hard body pressed against her softer one. But she was afraid. Would her emotions get out of control? Could she play at love and then walk away unscathed?

CHAPTER SIX

"Go to bed," he said softly.

Still she hesitated. She wished she dare agree to his outrageous plan. Wished she didn't feel so inadequate and uncertain. Wished most of all she didn't feel this pull of attraction with this sexy cowboy. He wasn't interested in her, not as a person. Yet she was interested in him. She didn't like it, but there it was.

"Tonight, at the country and western place, I met a lot of nice people. When I told them I was writing a romance novel, they had tons of ideas on what they considered romantic."

He watched her, his eyes steady and calm. Slowly he leaned against the back door and crossed his arms over his chest.

"And?"

"So, I thought maybe I should take a poll or something, find out what people find romantic and incorporate that in my book."

"You could, but I don't think you need to."

"Why not?" She was surprised.

"You're a woman, write what you find romantic."

"But what about what a man finds romantic?"

"I told you, I'm available for the time you're here."

"To tell me what you find romantic?"

He shrugged. "If you like. If that's all you want."

"I thought you wanted more."

"I do. But if you draw the line at words only, I'll abide by it. You have to make up your own mind, Maggie. I'm not going to do it for you."

That was a switch. She couldn't imagine her dad or Don saying that. She stared at him for another moment, knowing the next step had to come from her. And she knew what she wanted to do. Her senses clamored for him. She wanted to feel that electricity that charged through her whenever he touched her, wanted to revel in the sensations that lit her up like nothing else ever had. But she was wary of herself, and of Kyle. She hesitated.

"I could poll the men here on the ranch. Just ask questions."

"No."

She tilted her chin. "Why not?"

"Too disruptive."

"I'm not disruptive. I would just ask questions and note their answers."

"No."

"Give me a reason."

"I told you."

"If I spoke to them on their off time, I would not disrupt their work."

"No."

She wanted to scream in frustration. "You remind me of my father. Issuing edicts with no real reason to back them up. Very well, I won't ask any of the men anything while we are on the Rafter C."

He eyed her suspiciously. "Or off."

She smiled triumphantly. "You can't control our actions when we are away from the Rafter C. Next time Lance asks me to go into town with him, I'll go and ask him questions all the way there and back."

Kyle pushed away from the door and strode across the room to her. Excitement and anticipation shimmered just below the surface as Maggie held her ground, watching him storm over to her, his anger flaring at her provocative remarks. Did she want to provoke him?

"What's your game, Maggie? Are you trying my patience deliberately, or is it unintentional? Why are you here? You say you want to write a book and be on your way, yet you haven't sat down once as far as I can tell to do any work on it. And you flirt with my men, ask questions about the success of the ranch. What for? To test your femininity with these men? Or are you looking for a meal ticket?"

She shook her head, something dying inside her. He'd misinterpreted everything. "No," she whispered. "I want to write a book. In the meantime, I need to make a living. I was pushing, I'm sorry." How could she explain the urge that almost overwhelmed her to push and push until he gave? She didn't understand it herself, how could she made him understand?

"Go to bed," he repeated for the third time.

"Good night." She turned and hurried to her room before she gave in to the impulses that pounded through her. She had wanted his kiss, but without the agreement he'd asked for. She wasn't ready to make the kind of decision he demanded. Or was she?

Kyle watched her scurry away and frowned. She hadn't a clue how disruptive she could be. She upset his equilibrium every time he came around her. What was her real reason for taking the job? For being so damned provocative? He wanted her. More than he had wanted anyone in a long time. Yet he didn't trust her an inch. He had thought Jeannie honest and sincere, only to discover she'd been more interested in the money the ranch brought in than in building a life with him.

Maggie appeared different. Or was she? It didn't matter. If she agreed to his terms, they'd explore the sensuality between them and call it quits when she left. He liked being with her. He found her wide-eyed wonder at the things on the ranch refreshing. Even her daydreaming intrigued. He should be mad she wasn't better attuned to the real world, but he found it enchanting. Not the burned meals, or wet clothes, but the way she tuned everything out and gazed off into space. Her return to reality was always amusing.

He hoped she decided she wanted to gain some experience first-hand to use in her book. And he hoped she decided soon.

Though Saturday was technically her day off, and though she hadn't gone to bed until almost three o'clock, Maggie rose to fix breakfast at the usual time. She had not slept well. Maybe she'd take a nap that afternoon. In the meantime, she wanted breakfast; it didn't prove to be that much extra trouble to prepare it for everyone.

She cooked French toast and sausage, putting everything in the oven to keep warm. The men drifted in one at a time. Billy never did show up. Nor did Kyle. Maggie wondered where he was. Sleeping in? The others appreciated her efforts and thanked her.

Excited to have the rest of the day to herself, she cleaned up the kitchen and headed for the office. Turning on the computer, she pulled up the last chapter she had worked on and reread what she'd written. It seemed flat. Sighing, she began to edit, trying to get some spark that would reach out and grab her.

But she couldn't concentrate. Gazing out the window, she thought about all Kyle had said, and suggested. She didn't have much experience; maybe she should take him up on his offer. He had more experience than she did. Unbidden, Gillian's voice echoed in her mind. How friendly was Kyle with that Gillian? Had he made arrangements with Gillian for more dates? Where did that leave her? He had said he'd abide by her guidelines. Could she take what he had to offer and set some limits? Like, no going to bed together? She wanted love and some commitment before going that far. Yet his kisses inflamed her, set her cells spinning like nothing else ever had. She longed to ruffle his hair, trace those sleek muscles, taste him again.

And if she could capture some of the feelings that spilled through her every time he came near, she'd find the spark she missed in her book. It was time to make a decision. Did she want to live life to its fullest, or stay safe and secure as her father had taught her?

"The words won't type themselves," Kyle said, amusement lacing his voice.

She spun around, her heart beating rapidly at the mere sight of him. He looked wonderful.

"I was thinking."

"Yeah, I know." He walked into the office, his loose-legged gait like poetry in motion. His eyes never left hers. "If you want to see some of the ranch, come on. I'm riding out and you can go with me."

"Great!" Without a thought to her manuscript, she flicked off the computer and rose.

"I need to get my boots."

"Right. I'll meet you in the barn. Do you have a hat?" She shook her head.

"I'll find you one. Hurry up."

"Did you get breakfast?" she asked as she passed him on the way to the stairs.

"Yes. Thanks for fixing it. You didn't have to, Saturday is your day off."

"Wasn't much bother. I'll be right there." She ran up the stairs, her thoughts spinning. Kyle had asked her to go with him today. She would get to spend as much time with him as she wanted, and learn more about the Rafter C. Excitement spilled through her like warm wine. She could hardly wait.

In only a short time the two of them rode away from the homestead and out to the open range. The grass grew high, making a swishing sound as the horses walked through. The sky spread from horizon to horizon in a clear deep blue, the distant mountains shone brilliant in the morning sun. The air was still.

"It's beautiful," Maggie said breathlessly as she matched her horse's gait with Kyle's.

"I've never wanted to live anywhere else," Kyle acknowledged.

"Well, trust me, I've been all around and this is the prettiest place I've seen."

"Where is all around?"

"My dad is a contract consultant for the government. We've been in Washington, D.C., Virginia, Texas, Washington state and even California. Most recently Colorado."

"You must have moved a lot."

"Yes. When I get my own place, I'm staying put forever. I hate moving all the time, trying to make new friends, to fit in with people who have backgrounds I can never match. I guess I'm glad I got to see different areas of the country, but I don't suffer from wanderlust."

"My dad bought this place before he married. It's been in our family now for over thirty-five years. Except when I attended the university, I've lived here all my life. Can't imagine what it would be like to move frequently."

"It's not fun. You're lucky." Wistfully Maggie looked around. She would love to belong to a place like this. To know it had been in her family for years and would continue for generations to come.

"How well can you ride?" Kyle asked.

"I can stay on. Want to go faster?" She grinned at him. The day seemed brighter by being with him. Only the two of them and the endless open range.

"Yes." He urged his mount into a lope and Maggie kept up with him. The blood pounded through her veins, the wind blew past her face, cooling her heated skin. She felt so alive she tingled.

He drew up beneath a stand of cottonwood, near a pond. Slowing the horses, they walked quietly for a few minutes, then Kyle stopped and dismounted. He handed his reins to Maggie, his fingers brushing hers. "I need to check something." Walking deeper into the stand of trees, he studied the ground, the animal paths that led to the pond. He circled the pond and came back to Maggie.

"Looking for something?"

"Checking the tracks to make sure wolves haven't moved in on the range. They usually leave the grown cattle alone, but go after the calves."

"It's pretty here, hard to think about nature and the killer instinct of some of her creatures."

"All a part of life."

She nodded, her gaze caught with his. Her fingers felt numb holding his reins. Her heart caught in her throat. Mesmerized by his gaze, she could only look and hope he couldn't read the turmoil that raged through her.

"Maggie?"

"Yes?"

"Have you decided yet?" His low, sexy voice sent tendrils of sexual awareness shooting through to her fingers and toes.

She took a deep breath. Her whole life could be changed by a single word. Was she willing to chance it?

"Yes."

She tossed him the reins and quickly dismounted. Stepping closer, she raised a hand to his cheek. "I've decided it would be very nice to have some actual experience to draw upon to write my book." Just being with him would broaden her horizons. She would grab all the happiness she could now, save the memories for when she moved on.

He let his breath out slowly, as if he'd been holding it.

Her fingers trembled against his cheek and he covered her hand with his, holding her against the warmth and strength of his jaw. "I won't hurt you," he said gruffly.

She nodded, her eyes locked with his. He looked at her as if seeing her for the first time. Then a slow smile tilted the corners of his lips. "You're a pretty woman, Maggie Foster. That Don was a fool to let you get away."

Pleasure warmed her like the sun. She wished she could bottle the feeling to take out anytime she wanted. Smiling up at him, she knew nothing could mar the perfection of the day.

Slowly Kyle leaned forward until his breath brushed against her cheeks. She saw the desire in his eyes and her heart raced in anticipation. Slowly, as he drew even closer, her lids grew heavy and closed. Slowly, she felt his touch, light as a feather at first, pressing against her as he claimed her lips in a kiss that promised much.

He moved her hand to the back of his neck, released it and drew her against him in a tight embrace. His mouth moved against hers, teasing hers open, tracing her lips with his tongue before slipping inside the moist heat of her mouth to explore the shimmering waves of desire that jumbled in her.

Her hat fell off; she didn't notice. Her horse stomped impatiently; she didn't hear it. Her entire focus centered on Kyle's mouth, his body, the wondrous sensations he caused. Heat suffused, hotter than the Wyoming summer sun. Desire raged, stronger than the most compelling hunger. Delight bubbled up and rushed through her. And still he kissed her.

She held on for dear life. Feeling like she was spinning away in a vortex of light and heat and air, she held on to him to keep herself anchored on the earth. It was glorious. The most wonderful thing ever to happen to her.

Slowly, slowly, he ended the kiss, pulled back just an inch, still holding her soft compliant body against his. Her eyes opened and she gazed into the molten steel of his. Had the earth shifted on its axis, or was she the only one to feel like it had?

"That was nice," she said dreamily, knowing her cheeks must be flushed with the heat that poured through her.

"Nice?" He grinned. "Is that the best you can do? I don't think that's enough for your book. Should we practice some more? I'll kiss you, you tell me how you rate it. When you think you have enough for the book, we'll stop."

Her mind went blank. She couldn't *rate* his kisses. She could only feel the sensations so foreign as they captured her body and held her enthralled. If he thought she could think coherently after kissing her like that, he had a better opinion of her abilities than she did.

She took a deep breath to tell him so, but the scent of horses, grass, and Kyle's own masculinity threw her. She nodded and closed her eyes, opening her lips slightly for his next kiss. She would try to define exactly how she felt—

All good and well to plan to be analytical when being kissed. Until his mouth moved over hers, until his hands rubbed her back, moved around her ribs to cup the weight of her breasts and send shooting spirals of pure hunger deep in her body. She could not think, could not analyze, only feel. And the feelings were miraculous, amazing, truly amazing.

They were both breathing hard when he ended the kiss. "Well?"

"*Very nice.*"

He groaned and rested his forehead against hers. "What do I have to do to get beyond nice?"

She giggled softly and rubbed her nose against his. "I think it's me. I think you've fried my brains and I'm stuck on that word. Really, the kisses are better than nice. I've never been kissed so—nicely—in my life."

"When we get back to the house, I'm going to see if we have a thesaurus for you."

"You didn't think they were nice?" she asked in mock shock.

"No, I thought they were the knock-your-socks-off kind of kisses that have me wanting to rip this shirt off your body so I can feel your silky skin. I want to taste every inch of you, feel the weight of your breasts in my hands. See if my mouth on other parts of your body will drive me as wild as kissing your lips does."

She swallowed. The image he painted in her mind sprang up as clear as if he'd already done it. But everything moved too fast for her. For a second she was strongly tempted to give in, but knew she needed to keep some perspective.

Clearing her throat, she pulled back a little, as much as his strong arms would allow.

"Maybe we should slow down a bit," she said, searching his eyes. She didn't want to disappoint him, but there was only so much she could take. Agreeing to have an affair was a big step. She didn't want to do everything today.

"This is slow," he said.

"Not for me."

Sighing, he released her and reached over to get her hat. Gently he placed it on her head. "You're the boss. We'll go at whatever speed you want. But you have no one but yourself to blame if I become impatient. Kissing you is like setting fire to gasoline. I want to explode."

She beamed at him. "Kyle, you say the most marvelous things. I can use them in the book!"

He frowned. "I'm not saying them to have you write them in some book."

"But I thought this whole reason for having an affair was to help me with my book." Did he mean that? Was he speaking directly to her as a woman? Maggie didn't want to let the thought gain a foothold. She would set herself up for heartbreak if she did.

He brushed his thumb across her damp lips. "The idea is to give you some first-hand experience so your writing can be more realistic. But it's also to have a bit of fun along the way, for both you and me."

"Right." Her smile came from the heart. "I'm having fun."

"Sure, with *nice* kisses."

She nodded. "I'll try to come up with other adjectives, if that would make you feel better."

"No, I like knowing my kisses are only nice. Of course, I'll have to work on my technique. I would like a wonderful, or exciting sometime."

"They were wonderful."

"No changing things now. You said they were nice. I'll have to work harder, that's all."

The glow from their banter warmed her heart. Kyle's sense of fun surprised her. And pleased her. In addition to being the sexiest man she'd ever known, he could laugh at her and have her laugh with him. Did he have any idea what he did to her when he drew near? His teasing delighted her, and made her wish they could be friends forever. She wouldn't change things, but if her book didn't sell right away, maybe she could stay a bit longer at the Rafter C.

He pulled her hat down on her forehead. "Come on, Maggie, time to ride."

By the time they returned home, the sun sat low on the horizon. Kyle had shown her the cattle and the calves.

He'd explained roundups and branding, and how he culled the steers for market. Maggie had asked endless questions. While she wanted to learn every aspect of ranching, she also adored listening to his voice. She watched him talk, watched the love of his ranch shine through in his every word. And she basked in his attention.

"Thank you," she said as they reached the barn. "I had a wonderful day."

"Good. Go on inside and get cleaned up. I'll take care of your horse."

"I'll fix supper," she suggested, dismounting gingerly. Her legs felt like cooked spaghetti. Surreptitiously she clung to the saddle, hoping Kyle wouldn't notice. She bet Gillian rode hours every day and had no trouble once she dismounted.

She frowned. She didn't want to think about his girlfriend after the day they'd spent together. Not after the kisses they'd shared. Not after the agreement they'd struck.

He took the reins and nodded. "Something light. The men will have already eaten."

"Soup and sandwiches?" she suggested, testing her knees. She thought they would hold her.

"Peanut butter again?"

Raising her nose in the air, she let go of the saddle and headed for the house, turning at the last minute and giving him a disdainful look. "I make wonderful peanut butter sandwiches, you should be so lucky to have me make you some."

He chuckled and headed for the barn.

Maggie waited until he entered before turning back toward the house. She'd take a quick shower and then fix them something. Only the two of them, it would be a nice dinner. Grimacing at the word, she vowed she would come up with a whole vocabulary of spectacular adjectives to use in the future. She felt more than nice about the whole situation.

By the time she showered and donned fresh clothes, Maggie ached with fatigue, so tired she could scarcely see straight. The lack of sleep the night before combined with the hard riding they'd done today made her wonder if she could stay awake long enough to eat dinner. But she didn't want to miss any time with Kyle, not after the start to their affair today. And after dinner she might just take him up on that offer to find a thesaurus.

Maggie thought to have a quiet dinner *à deux*, but she had underestimated the draw of the house to the cowboys. While they had all grabbed something to eat, Jack came to the kitchen for coffee, Billy came by to see if there was anything for dessert. Trevor and Pete wandered in to see what kept the other two.

Giving up, Maggie finished her dinner, put her plate in the dishwasher and wandered down to the office. If Kyle wanted to talk with his men, she'd work on her book. Flicking on her computer, she sat down with the best of intentions. But as she stared blankly at the words on the screen, she knew she wouldn't get anything done tonight. She was too tired to see straight, much less be creative.

It was comfortable in the old house. In the background she could hear the rumble of the men's voices. Outside the wind blew gently, rustling the leaves of the cottonwoods. The clock on the wall by the door ticked softly. Maybe she'd close her eyes for just a second. If she didn't feel more awake soon, she'd give up and go to bed.

"Maggie?" Kyle shook her gently.

Slowly she lifted her lids and gazed at him. "What?" Blinking as she tried to wake up, Maggie glanced around. She was still in the office.

"Go to bed, Maggie. You're asleep at your desk," he said softly.

"I'll never get this book written at this rate," she complained.

"You can do some more work tomorrow. It's Sunday. Take the whole day to work on your book. No meals for anyone but yourself."

She smiled. She wanted her hero to be just like Kyle, with his sexy voice, his killer smile and his gentle touch.

"Come on, Maggie." He scooped her up from the chair and carried her from the room.

"I could walk," she said, encircling his neck with her arms and resting her head against his shoulder. Closing her eyes, she relished the sensation of being carried. No one had ever done that for her before. "Aren't I heavy?"

"Yeah, you weigh a ton," he said, chuckling.

She pulled back at that. "Put me down!"

"So you can fall asleep on your feet?" he asked, beginning to climb the stairs.

"I didn't sleep very well last night." She gave up her token struggle and rested her head against his, closing her eyes, burrowing into the warmth of his shoulder.

"And we had a full day today."

"Mmm." Full and wonderful.

He pushed open her door and crossed the room to lay her on the bed. Maggie kept her eyes closed while Kyle pulled off her shoes and pulled a comforter over her.

"See you in the morning," he said.

She smiled, turned to her side and promptly fell back asleep.

Kyle stared down at her for a long moment, struck by the trusting way she slept. He thought back to Jeannie, and how she had calculated every move. At the time he had thought her carefree and fun, but in retrospect he saw how she had manipulated things to go exactly the way she wanted. If he hadn't found her in the arms of that other man, he might have gone through with the wedding. If he hadn't heard her admit money was more important than anything, he might have been tempted to listen to her when she tried to explain the passionate embrace he interrupted.

Was Maggie capable of such manipulation? He hadn't seen anything to suggest it, but she was a woman. It would be a long time before he trusted someone with his heart, if ever. And when the time came, he wanted a woman he could depend on. Someone more like his mother than this flighty daydreaming woman. His mother hadn't forgotten to dry clothes, she hadn't burned meals, or prepared insubstantial amounts. And she sure hadn't gone off into another world when she had work to do.

He hoped Maggie'd get started on her book tomorrow. The sooner she finished it and left, the sooner life would settle down again.

Kyle left the room without a backward look. The desire he felt around her didn't diminish. Her kisses were a curious mix of innocence and sensual provocation. Her wide-eyed wonder at the love play between them made him feel like some sort of superhero, yet he knew where that could lead, if he believed it. She was here temporarily, and he was willing to play while she stayed. But it would end when she left. And if she didn't get her act together, that leaving might come sooner than either one suspected.

CHAPTER SEVEN

MAGGIE woke late the next morning. Knowing it was her one remaining free day for the week, she took her time getting dressed, donning a denim skirt and soft, cotton, pink scooped-neck shirt. She wore sandals instead of her usual tennis shoes. She didn't plan to go out to the barn, and if she wanted to take a walk later, she'd go on the paved driveway.

By the time she ventured downstairs it was drawing close to noon. The house sounded empty. She fixed herself some toast and tea, ate, then wandered around the first floor looking for Kyle. He was not there. Not that she cared. She just wondered where he had gone. Didn't he take a day off? Was he out on the range, or just in the barn? Didn't matter. She would not seek him out.

Wandering into the office, she opened the window to enjoy the fresh air while she worked. On her desk lay a thesaurus. Warily, she sat down and drew it toward her. A bookmark stuck up between the pages and she turned to find the word *nice* underlined. She smiled slowly when she saw the bold handwritten notes in the margin. *See stupendous, mind-boggling, glorious, fantastic, phenomenal, extraordinary*. Stunned, she stared at the bold handwriting. Was that the way he saw her kisses, or thought she should see his?

If the latter, he was right, his kisses had been fantastic. Gazing out the window, she could clearly remember every second of each kiss they'd shared beneath the trees yesterday. Heart-pumping, toe-tingling kisses

106

unlike any she had ever experienced. Her body tingled in response twenty-four hours later. The gentle breeze stirring cooled her heated cheeks. Her eyes closed as she relived their ride. Sighing softly, she opened them. Enough time spent on memories. She had work to do.

She began to type. She would put her heroine in the same kind of situation with the hero. Could she express on paper the kind of emotions she felt? Express so the world would understand the feelings that clamored for more of his touch, more kisses? Could she capture the beauty of the day, how the sun had warmed the air and ground, how the breeze had skimmed across her cheeks, cooling the heat his touch raised? Could she put down in black and white the feelings that threatened to overwhelm her when he drew her into his embrace, when his warm gray eyes threatened to swamp her good sense with the desire so evident until she could see it with her own eyes closed?

She wanted to. But how could she put into words the wonder that had engulfed her? Staring out the window, her mind saw them together in the shade of the big cottonwoods, Kyle's hands tracing patterns of delight against her back, his mouth demanding a response from hers that she had never before given.

The clock chimed softly. Maggie glanced its way, then back to the screen. She'd been there over an hour and not written a single paragraph. Sighing, she began to type once again, trying to infuse her story with the delights she'd experienced.

But at the back of her mind hovered the constant wonder of where Kyle had gone. From the conversation she heard in the kitchen last night, the men weren't working today. Had Kyle ridden out to check something? Or, the unbidden thought crept in, had he gone to see Gillian?

Restless, she took a break and went to the kitchen for a glass of water. As she drank, she noticed the blue and white truck was gone from its usual spot by the barn. Kyle must have taken it. Sighing softly, she put the glass on the counter and wandered out onto the front porch. She wished she knew if he had gone into town to see that Gillian. How long had he known her? Was she pretty? Was she waiting patiently for Kyle to get over his former fiancée's betrayal, ready to step right up when he wanted to love again?

And why not? He had a perfect right to see whomever he wished. He had made no commitment to her. And Maggie wasn't staying for long. Yet she found it hard to hold on to the thought. She didn't like thinking that his wild kisses meant nothing. Though he'd been upfront with her that their affair would be of short duration, lasting only as long as she remained on the ranch, he had not said anything about seeing only her. Did he feel footloose and fancy free, able to come and go as he saw fit? *Had he gone to see Gillian?* After yesterday, Maggie had hoped she'd be enough female companionship to satisfy him. Did he find her so lacking he had to go elsewhere?

It was peaceful on the porch. She sat back in a rocker, pushing it back and forth. Occasionally she heard a muffled thump when one of the horses in the corral kicked away a fly. She could see for miles, endless stretches of green pasture, with the silhouette of the Snowy Range to the west white against the azure sky. The steady motion of the rocker soothed jangled nerves. Slowly her mind began another exploration of her feelings around Kyle Carstairs. She remained lost in daydreams for a long time.

Kyle turned onto the driveway for the Rafter C, in a bad mood. It was getting late and he'd spent the day in

Laramie, visiting his sister and her husband, Jake. He'd left to get away from Maggie, to give her the day free to write on her book. And to give them some time apart. While physically he might desire her, he didn't want her getting the wrong idea about a relationship between them. It was strictly a short-term affair.

But he hadn't counted on thinking about her all day long. The drive over had been bad enough, though he had played the radio loudly trying to drown out her image that popped up tirelessly. But when Angel cross-examined him on the new housekeeper, he found himself thinking of Maggie even more. Fortunately, Jake had headed his wife off from her relentless questioning and for part of the afternoon Kyle had put thoughts of Maggie aside. Until he headed for home.

Drawing up into the yard, his anger flared. When he had thought of Maggie during the day he'd envisioned her working on her book, spending the entire day at her computer. Instead, he pulled up into the yard near a group of his men, leaning on the corral fence, watching as Billy did some trick riding. The stock horses had been moved from the corral, only Billy and his gelding remained, showing off. Maggie stood in the midst of the men, laughing at Billy's antics. And right next to her stood Lance McCord.

At the sound of the truck, Maggie turned. Seeing Kyle drive in, her heart kicked. She smiled and waved, then turned back to Billy lest someone guess how glad she was that Kyle was home. Her heart beat faster as she threw a smile toward Lance. She didn't want Kyle to suspect how much she missed him. Yet the air seemed clearer, the smell of dust and horse and hay stronger. Every sensation sharpened. She heard the door slam behind him and in only seconds he'd joined her by the rail.

"Get much writing done?" he asked laconically, glancing at Lance.

Lance looked over, his eyes narrowed, while Maggie nodded.

"A bit."

"Thought you'd still be at your computer," Kyle continued, holding on to his temper with real effort.

"Nope, finished for now. I'm taking a break."

His eyes traveled down the length of her, taking in her bare arms and the low neck of her shirt, her short skirt, her long tanned legs, the ridiculous sandals she wore, the pink polish on her toenails.

"Not dressed for a ranch," he said, his eyes resting on the tempting expanse of her fair skin just above her neckline.

"I think she looks great," Lance said, smiling at Maggie, shifting slightly to close the distance between them.

Kyle's head jerked up and he glared at his foreman. "Not suitable for a ranch. Her feet are already dirty from the dust."

Maggie looked up at him, then down at her dusty feet. Kyle was right, but why be so adamant? So she'd have to wash her feet, big deal. She turned back to watch Billy, aware of the tension radiating from Kyle. She had hoped he would like to see her in a skirt. She'd worn jeans since she arrived.

"They'll wash. I think she looks great," Lance said, reaching out to smooth a lock of Maggie's hair around one finger, rubbing it with his thumb.

Kyle knocked his hand away, yanking her hair.

"Ow!" Maggie turned to glare at him.

The men turned their attention to Kyle and Lance, forgetting Billy temporarily. Two of them shuffled back and leaned against the fence.

"Lance, don't you have something else to do?" Kyle asked in a dangerously low voice.

Lance smiled and shook his head. "Nope. This is Sunday, my day off. I'm just enjoying myself."

Kyle glanced around at the faces of the other men. They were attuned to the scene playing out before them and one or two were obviously confused.

"Come with me." Kyle wrapped his hand around Maggie's bare arm and headed for the house.

"What's up?" she asked, skipping a step trying to keep up. "Is something wrong?" Besides her own heart rate that threatened to race out of control. His hand was hot and hard, the shimmering waves of sensation that shot through her from his touch disturbing.

"I thought you were going to write today. I left you alone all day so you'd have plenty of time for writing, and what do I find when I get back but you're out there flirting with every man on the place."

She set her feet and jerked them to a stop, wincing as his hand tightened on her arm. "Wait a minute, Kyle Carstairs. I wasn't flirting with anyone! I simply took a break and came outside. I've written over a dozen pages today, a good output from me. But I got blurry-eyed at the computer and when I went outside for a walk, Billy sat there bragging about some kind of tricks he could do on his horse, so I went to watch. Just because the others watched, too, hardly counts as flirting!"

"What about the way you're dressed?"

"What's wrong with the way I'm dressed?" She glanced down. The pink shirt looked clean, despite leaning against the corral rail. The blue denim skirt had creased across her lap from sitting all day, but there was nothing wrong with it.

"These men work hard all week, and on the weekend are ready to let loose. A couple of them have girlfriends, but the rest play the field. And, honey, you look ready to play." His forefingers traced the neckline of her shirt, skimming across the soft swells of her breasts like a hot brand.

She slapped his hand away and looked furtively toward the corral. The men were watching Billy, except for Lance, who watched Kyle and her. His smile could be seen from where she stood.

She looked at Kyle, furious at his insinuations. "I can dress the way I want."

"Not while you work for me, you can't. Either put on some clothes, or pack up and leave."

She stared at him in total surprise. "Kyle? Are you nuts?" There was nothing wrong with her clothes. Why did he insist on making such a big deal of it?

His dark gray eyes gazed back into hers for a long time. Finally, he nodded. "Not nuts, only very serious."

She felt like a child again, with her father dictating to her with no rhyme or reason given. Now Kyle thought he could order the way she dressed. She shook off his hold on her arm and turned to the house, her head held high. She would not be dictated to, no matter what. Slowly she climbed the steps to the back porch, opened the door, feeling as if she were caught up in some nightmare. Why did men think they had the right to boss her around like she was some half-wit?

She was twenty-three years old, full grown, and totally capable of taking care of herself. She tossed her head and headed for the stairs. She could be packed and gone within the hour. She refused to consider where she would go so late on a Sunday night. He still owed her for the week's work, that would be enough to get a motel room somewhere. First thing tomorrow, she'd have to find another job.

She pulled her empty suitcases from beneath her bed and began to load her clothes in them.

"What are you doing?" Kyle stood in the open door. She hadn't heard him follow her.

She glanced over, resumed unloading the dresser drawer. "It should be obvious, I'm packing."

"Just change your clothes. Don't leave."

"You know, Kyle, you never did finish telling me why the other housekeepers left. Did you dictate what they could wear, too?"

"No, I didn't need to. They had more sense than to wear provocative clothing."

She slammed down the lid on one suitcase and turned to him, anger flaring. "I'm not wearing anything provocative!"

"You look as provocative as hell," he roared.

Her eyes widened and she stared at him, anger fleeing as quickly as it had come. He found her provocative? In her denim skirt and cotton shirt?

"Are you crazy?" she whispered, stunned at the thought.

"Maybe." He took a step into her room, his eyes never wavering from hers. "It's bad enough during the week when you wear those snug jeans that display every inch of your rounded bottom and long legs. Do you know how many times I've wanted to reach out and touch you, jeans and all? Now you have a short skirt that shows almost every inch of those long legs of yours. Your skin looks as soft as rose petals. Do you have any idea how much I want to touch you?"

She noticed his hands were clenched into fists. To keep from reaching out to her? She caught her breath, her heart slamming against her ribs. Her skin tingled all over. She opened her mouth to refute what he said, but he spoke before she could.

"What would the bare skin of your arms feel like wrapped around my neck? You've hugged me before, but always wearing sleeves. And that damned neckline, it's too low. I can see the beginning swells of your breasts, the hint of a shadow between them." His eyes locked with hers and Maggie saw the burning heat.

She swallowed hard, trying to escape his gaze, unable to move a muscle.

"And the top is too loose. Remember how I held you yesterday beneath the cottonwoods? I remember every inch of your delectable body, and I could so easily slip my hands up beneath that top and trace every inch of you."

As if in a daze, Maggie slowly took a step closer, another. Her eyes held his, her heart raced, the blood heating through her veins. His words were like nectar to a dying man. No one had ever waxed so poetic about her before in her life. Never. Maggie halted mere inches from him, her head tipped back to maintain eye contact. Kyle groaned softly and reached for her. He pulled her tightly against him and just held her, his head dropping to find her mouth, claim her lips with his own. Sealing them both in a world of touch and feel and exploding sensations.

Her bare arms wrapped around his neck as Maggie opened her mouth and welcomed him.

His hand roamed over her back, down to cup the curve of her bottom, lifting her slightly against him, snuggling her close. Then one hand slipped beneath the loose top, tracing the long line of her spine, dipping beneath the waistband of her skirt, back up to find and unfasten her bra. Slowly, Kyle eased her away enough to bring his hand around her ribs, slowly, ever so slowly, up to cup the weight of her breast.

She sighed into his mouth and pressed against him. The fiery conflagration he built threatened to overwhelm her, to sweep her away. She wanted to smile at the delight that pierced her, but she dare not release his mouth for a second. It was heaven on earth and she wanted to savor every bit of it.

When his thumb brushed across her nipple she whimpered and arched into him, seeking more attention, seeking more of him.

Kyle broke the kiss to trail a string across her cheek, along her jaw, down to the pounding pulse point at the base of her throat. He brushed his thumb against her again as Maggie became almost frantic. She arched her body against his as if trying to bury herself in him, whimpering in frantic demanding need.

"Shh," Kyle whispered, moving to nip her earlobe, soothe it with his tongue. "Easy, baby, easy. Slow down." He slid his hand around to her back, rubbing her as he would gentle a fractious horse.

Maggie clung to him, to keep from falling, her cheek against his, her arms tight around his neck. She clenched her eyes tightly and tried to get her breathing under control, tried to stop the roiling sensations that racked her. She knew he wanted her. He had told her more than once, and she could feel the evidence against her belly. Why had he stopped?

His hands were like hot brands on the bare skin of her back. She burned from the heat they generated. She hated to part from him, but nothing had changed. Perplexed, she wondered why he'd kissed her.

"Are you all right?" he asked softly.

She nodded. "But I don't think I know what's going on," she said against his ear. She kissed his cheek then drew back so she could see into his eyes.

"Nothing's going on. Just change your clothes."

She frowned. "Kyle, I won't be dictated to." Pushing away, she spun around and crossed her arms over her chest, trying to retain some of the warmth of their embrace.

"I'm not dictating anything," he almost roared.

She turned back. "You are, too. You ordered me to either change my clothes to suit your idea of propriety, or get out. I won't be told what to do. I had a lifetime of that with my father and Don."

"Hell." He ran one hand through his hair, and moved across to the window.

Maggie watched him, hoping he would say something to change things. Afraid he never would. She eyed her suitcases. Might as well finish packing. She reached up under her shirt to refasten her bra just as he turned.

"I can do that." Kyle stepped across to her.

"I can manage."

Ignoring her, he reached behind, tangled with her fingers, then found the ends of her bra. In seconds he had it fastened. His fingers lingered for a second, skimming the soft skin, then pulling her shirt down.

"I didn't mean to come across like your dad or ex-fiancé," he said. "I don't feel anything like your father."

She stared at him a long time. "It's because of Jeannie, isn't it? You're objecting to the way I dress because of her. Something about me reminds you of her."

He remained quiet for so long, she didn't think he would respond. Then he sighed and nodded. "She's the reason I don't want you to dress like that. Why I want you to stay away from the men. Especially dressed like that."

"Jeannie dressed provocatively," Maggie guessed shrewdly.

He nodded. "That and more."

"More?"

He nodded and turned back to the window, moving until he could lean against the sill. "I told you Jeannie wanted the money from the ranch, not the owner."

"Yes." She watched him warily. A hint of trepidation crept in.

"But I didn't tell you how I found out."

She shook her head, but he didn't see her. He gazed out over the range. Or was he looking back several years?

"I came home early one day from a cattle sale, thinking to celebrate the sale with Jeannie. She had been staying for the week. I came upstairs and found her in bed with one of my ranch hands."

"Oh, God." Shocked, Maggie didn't know what to say.

"I heard them as I climbed the stairs. So I made sure I didn't make any noise once I suspected what was going on. They had left the door open." Kyle fell silent for a moment.

Maggie stepped closer. She wanted to reach out and touch him, offer some kind of support, but she didn't know if he'd want it or not. He looked completely self-sufficient standing at the window. Was it a facade?

"They were laughing and talking, about how she would have lots of money once she married me and if they were discreet they could continue to see each other. I think she was completely floored when I appeared in the doorway and spoke."

Maggie reached out and covered one clenched fist with her own hand. She wished she could do something to ease his pain. "I'm sorry," she said.

"Yeah, I was, too." He took a deep breath and turned to look at her. "Not only did I lose my fiancée, but one of the best hands that worked here. And made two others so upset they left, as well. I won't put up with the same kind of disruption that caused. I have asked you and told you to stay away from the men. Do you understand why?"

She nodded. "Not only do I understand, I can agree with your reasoning. Why not explain at the beginning?"

"It really wasn't any of your business," he said coolly.

Maggie felt as if she'd been slapped. She released her hold on his hand and stepped back. "Of course, you are correct. It wasn't then and it isn't now. Thank you, however, for explaining it to me. Once I have an explanation, I can comply with rules and regulations. It's the arbitrary and capricious ones I can't handle."

"Maggie, I—"

"No, you were well within your rights as boss to request I dress appropriately. I'll change now. If you'll excuse me." She looked away, her chin held high. She felt the sting of embarrassment at his cold rejoinder, but she would not give way. If he would just get out of her room she could change into the jeans and long-sleeved shirts he found acceptable. And stay the hell away from him in the future. She'd give no cause for future complaints!

"You'll stay?"

"Yes. I'll dress in jeans from now on. I need to stay a little longer." She had nowhere else to go. She'd given up her apartment, had no other job lined up. Maybe this was a warning to make contingent plans. She was at the total mercy of this man. If he fired her instantly, she had nowhere else to go. Not a good position to be in.

"I'll see you downstairs, then." He crossed her room. Maggie waited until she heard his boots on the stairs before following him to close her door. It was her day off and she had no responsibilities around the ranch. She'd sneak down later and get something to eat, but for as long as she could, she would avoid Kyle Carstairs.

She unpacked, his cold words echoing in her mind. *It was none of your business.* True. Why did it hurt so much? Had she expected more because of his kisses? He had offered to give her some sexual experience to aid in the writing of her book. He was attracted to her, as she was to him, but that was all. Sexual attraction. It meant nothing more to him, obviously. And it would mean nothing more to her!

She pulled on an old cotton shirt, buttoning it to her neck, fastening the cuffs. She found a pair of jeans that were a bit big and put them on, remembering his comment about her jeans. Maybe she should get several pairs that were baggy. Brushing off her dusty feet, she lay down on her bed and stared at the ceiling and thought about all Kyle had told her.

God, Maggie made him so mad sometimes he wanted to shake her! She had been ready to leave, just because he ordered her to wear jeans. She could have asked for the reason. He stormed into the office and yanked out his chair. Plopping down in it, he glared at her computer, the terminal still blinking. She would drive a saint crazy!

He tilted back in the chair and glanced up toward the ceiling. Was she changing her clothes? Or had she decided to give up and pack? He wished— He didn't know which he wished. She tied him in knots and he didn't like it one bit. She was just a temporary housekeeper, and not a very good one at that. Maybe she should leave. She had enough experience with kisses now to write a book on that alone. And if he didn't cool things down, he could push her farther than she wanted to go, as in all the way, with naked bodies tumbling in bed, and hot kisses everywhere.

As the minutes ticked by, and it remained silent upstairs, Kyle grew impatient. Maybe he had come on a bit strong, but the image of Jeannie and Walt Hamilton wouldn't go away. Kyle had seen Lance's attitude around Maggie. He didn't want Lance and Maggie involved. If it came to that, he'd have to let them both go. And Lance was too good a foreman to lose.

Would she stay away from Lance now that she knew the reason he'd requested it? Would she stay away from him? Where was she? He rose and walked into the hall.

Glancing up the stairs, he saw the closed door. For a moment he considered storming up and demanding she open it so he could see her again. But he held off. Something told him he'd done enough for one day.

Turning back to the office he crossed to her computer. If she'd finished for the day, he should shut it off. But he hesitated, drawn to the words displayed on the screen. Slowly he sat before the monitor and read the sentences. Pressing the arrow key, he moved back to the beginning and began to read.

He shook his head. He had never read a romance novel, but he had read plenty of fiction. He didn't think the quality of writing for romance would be any less. But her writing wasn't very good. The characters were stick figures. There was no emotion. The movements were jerky and artificial. And it broke his heart. She wanted to write so much, had such glowing plans for when she became published. If this was a sample, he knew she had a long way to go.

When he got to the passage where the hero kisses the heroine for the first time, he slowed down, reread it. It showed promise. At least she didn't call it *nice*. Maybe her lack of experience held her back. He wondered if the couple in the book would have a fight, like they'd had a few minutes ago. How would they react, would they make up or stay mad?

He was curious as to how she planned to handle the story, and if she could make it come alive. When he reached the end, he saved everything in case she had not yet done so, and turned off the computer. Sitting at the chair she used, gazing out the open window, he wondered if the fact the hero resembled him was coincidence or not. She had started the book before she arrived at the Rafter C, but the man sure sounded like him. Or a nicer Kyle, more how a woman might want a man. Was she using him for more than just a means to garner experience? Was she patterning everything for the hero on his life? How long would it take her to finish the book, mail it off and learn its fate? How long was she staying?

It was dark by the time Maggie crept down the stairs. She didn't see Kyle, so she went into the kitchen to fix herself a sandwich. Pouring a large glass of ice tea, she took her makeshift meal and headed back to her room. At the bottom of the steps, his voice stopped her.

"Come eat out on the porch, Maggie. The evening's nice, there's no wind tonight."

She hesitated. It would be safer in her room. Did she want to beard the lion once more before the day ended?

"Maggie?" The voice beguiled, entreated. Or was it her imagination? He sounded as he always did.

"Okay." She turned and went out onto the porch. Kyle held the door for her. "Did you eat?" she asked as she sat down carefully in a rocker.

"A while ago. I got a sandwich, too. My sister fixed a big meal at lunch."

"That's where you were today?" So he hadn't been with Gillian. For no reason at all, she felt a small weight lift from her shoulders.

"I went into Laramie to see her and her new husband."

"The man you told to stay away from her," Maggie clarified.

"Yeah. Only that was before they were married. Obviously he didn't listen to me."

"Are they happy?"

"Very. An afternoon around them is all I can take," Kyle said wryly. He didn't begrudge his sister her happiness. He just didn't expect the same thing for himself.

She nibbled on her sandwich, knowing he had once thought to be happily married by now to Jeannie. No wonder he didn't want to be around his sister. It must hurt. She felt it sometimes herself. She had thought to get married and have a life-style far different from that of her father's. Yet the only man to ask her, the only man she'd thought she loved, had proved to be too similar. While she sometimes envied other people's happiness, she tried to remain patient. Someday love might come for her. And if not, at least she had her writing.

"And your brother is married, too, isn't he?" she asked as the silence grew.

"Yes. To a little bit of a woman who has him wrapped completely around her little finger. He's crazy about her."

"That's nice." Maggie smiled. She wished she could find a man to wrap around her little finger. Someone who would want to please her all the time. Or at least treat her like an adult and not order her around to suit his needs.

"Rafe seems to like it."

"But you wouldn't?"

"Probably not."

"Do they come to the ranch a lot? Didn't you say you all own it jointly?"

"We do. Rafe and Charity come by in the fall. They usually attend some of the home football games at the university, and then stay the rest of the weekend here. Angel comes most summers for a few weeks. I don't know her plans for this summer. She and Jake just got married a couple of months ago."

"Even though they have ownership interest, you really run the place, don't you?"

"Are you interested in me as a man, Maggie, or as the hero for your book?" he asked suddenly.

She almost choked on a bit of tuna. "My book?" Dread and alarm reared up.

"I read it while you were upstairs."

"You read my book?" She threw the rest of the sandwich on the plate. "You had no business reading my manuscript. It's a long way from finished and I don't want anyone reading it until it is."

"Too late, I read it. I'm not sure I like the hero."

CHAPTER EIGHT

"Isn't that why you're writing it, for others to read?" Kyle asked.

"It's not finished yet."

He shrugged. "You left the computer on. I read the display."

"Next time exercise a little control and stay away from my computer!" Maggie bit her lip, unsure of the emotions that his words evoked. "How did you like it?" she asked, at last. Her first critic. She held her breath waiting for him to reply.

Kyle hesitated.

"It's awful, isn't it?" she moaned. Damn, she knew it wasn't ready to submit, but was it so bad he couldn't find anything positive to say?

"It's a bit wooden. As if you don't know how to draw the characters so they show depth. And the scene where he kisses her is bland."

"I just haven't reached my stride yet," she mumbled, disappointed he hadn't liked what she'd done so far.

"Come on." Kyle stood up and held open the screen door.

"Where?" Maggie rose and entered the house. His hand at the small of her back guided her down the hall to the office.

Kyle snapped on the light and led her to her computer. Taking the plate from her, he put it near the edge of the table. Pressing on her shoulders, he sat her in the chair, reaching across her to flip on her computer.

"Bring up the kiss scene," he said, drawing another chair closer and sitting beside her.

Her face warm with heat, Maggie complied, her eyes scanning the words. Bland and boring and not at all like what she wanted to portray. Not at all like the pictures in her head. Why couldn't she get it right?

"Now, look this way," he said.

She turned obediently.

Kyle smiled at her and cupped her chin. Lightly brushing his lips across hers, he pulled back and looked at her.

"How was that?"

"Fine."

"No, how do you feel?"

Her heart pounded as if she had run a race, her chin tingled from his touch, her eyes were dazzled by the sight of him. She used all her willpower to keep her hands gripping the arms of the chair. She wanted to reach out for him, hold him tightly against her and drown in his kisses.

"Breathless?" she asked.

He cocked an eyebrow and smiled. "Write that down."

"What?"

"Write down the kiss and what you feel." He released her chin and sat back, watching her.

Conscious of his gaze on her, Maggie turned to the computer and tried to capture the feelings of that brief touch of his lips against hers, and the riot of sensations it caused. Her fingers felt clumsy. She kept hitting the wrong keys, but gradually she tapped out the words that closely mirrored how she felt from his kiss.

"Next one," Kyle said.

"Next one what?" She turned to look over her shoulder.

"Next kiss." He turned her to face him and lowered his mouth to hers. Gently moving against her lips, he teased her, drawing his tongue along the seam, nipping gently at her lower lip when she opened to him. All too soon he sat back, a satisfied expression gleaming in his eyes.

"Write how you feel."

Maggie stared at the screen, unable to think. Slowly her fingers began to type the words that tried to express the heat that simmered in her veins, the yearning for more that filled her being; the delightful awareness, the increased sensitivity being with Kyle generated.

Finally the words came to a halt.

"Next one."

She took a deep breath. Anticipation bubbled through her like fine wine. How many more kisses would there be? If each got more erotic, she would be so dazed she wouldn't be able to type. Eagerly she swiveled her chair and gazed up at him.

"Next one," she confirmed.

He studied her for a long moment, the heat in his eyes ignited her. She watched as his hands came up to slowly thread through her silky hair. When he tilted her head back and took in the length of her neck, her jawline, the answering fire in her eyes, Maggie grew impatient. She wanted more. Slowly Kyle smiled and drew her even closer for his kiss. His breath mingled with hers as he held his lips scant millimeters from hers.

"Kyle," she entreated.

"Anticipation adds spice," he murmured, touching his tongue to the corner of her mouth.

Maggie tried to lean closer, but his hands held her exactly where he wanted her.

"Not yet."

"Yes," she whispered, her hands coming up to clasp around his wrist, tugging him closer.

"You always smell like roses. Is it your hair, or your body, or the essence of you?" he asked, skimming hot kisses along her jaw.

She moaned softly and closed her eyes to better savor the exquisite delights that sparkled through her.

"Are you taking note of every feeling so you can put it in your book?" he asked as his lips touched hers.

Before she could reply, he deepened the kiss, opening her mouth and searching the warmth he found with his tongue.

Maggie lost track of time and place and self, absorbed by the fiery heat that built from his mouth to hers. Her body ached for his touch. His hands kneading her scalp weren't enough, she wanted to feel him against her, revel in the pleasure her body took from his. To know the differences between them that his hard frame suggested when pressed against her softer one.

"Write about that," he said, breathing erratically.

Maggie shook her head, nothing cleared the spinning sensation. She glanced at the computer screen, then back at Kyle. Half rising, she moved from her chair to his lap and encircled his neck with her arms. "You're kidding, right?" she said, trailing kisses along his cheek, feeling the rough abrasion of his day-old whiskers. "I could no more type a word than I could ride a bronc right now." Her mouth moved to his and she sighed in relief when he pulled her tightly against his chest and resumed their kiss.

His hands moved over her rounded hips, down the outer side of her thighs. Breaking off to mumble against her lips, he complained about her changing her skirt.

She giggled. "It was an order, as I recall."

"Damn fool order," he said, kissing her neck, licking the pulse point at its base. Moving one hand to the front, he slowly began to unfasten her buttons. "I liked your other shirt better."

"That's not what you said a little while ago," she murmured, nipping his earlobe. One hand threaded through his thick hair while the other mimicked his as she began to release the buttons on his shirt.

His mouth claimed hers again, ending the talk. When Maggie felt the cool night air on her skin, she knew she was losing her shirt. Kyle moved to unfasten her bra.

"No." She sat up and held her hand across her breasts. Blinking in the light, she stared at him, uncertainty evident in her eyes. His shirt hung halfway off his shoulder, opened to the waist. His bronzed skin shone in the lamplight. And her eyes dropped to gaze on the tantalizing expanse of masculine chest.

"Just this, no more," he urged, his fingers releasing the fastening and drawing the bra down her arms. Slowly Maggie moved her hand and let him toss the scrap of lace and silk across the room. He took her hands and drew them away from her body while he looked at her. Then, so slowly she hardly knew she moved, he drew her to him. Breast to chest, soft to hard, warmth to heat.

"You're a pretty lady, Maggie Foster," he whispered in her ear, his hands caressing the strong muscles of her back.

"You are one gorgeous, sexy cowboy, Kyle Carstairs," she replied, relishing the sensations that poured through her. She felt every inch of him pressed against her, could even feel the pounding of his heart beneath her breast. She tightened her arms, wanting to be even closer, wanting to be a part of him.

"Remember how you feel for your book," he said.

"I'll remember." But not for the book, for herself. She would never forget how wonderful everything felt. How right she felt in his lap, moving her body against his, learning more of what it meant to be a woman. There was no one like Kyle in the world, and she loved it. Loved him.

For a moment, she caught her breath, stilled like a doe caught in headlights. Then she smiled and relaxed against him. No wonder she liked his kisses, liked having him touch her. She loved him! It was right to enjoy demonstrating that affection.

And she wanted more. She wanted to learn all he had to teach her. And show him how much she loved him.

When he deepened the kiss, she responded fully. Imprinting every single nuance to the embrace, she knew she would never forget the night as long as she lived.

When he moved to kiss her shoulder, she smiled, relishing the tingling sensation his mouth made against her skin.

"I love you," she whispered, her heart so full.

He reacted as if she'd thrown cold water on him. He sat up and gripped her upper arms, pushing her away from him until he could see her clearly.

"What did you say?" His voice was cool, his eyes angry and narrowed.

Maggie stared at him, startled at his response. "I love you," she faltered.

"Oh, no, you don't. Don't confuse sex with love," he said, his hands biting into her arms.

"I'm not. I think I've been falling in love with you since I got here."

"I don't believe this. You came here to work, not make a play for me."

"I'm not making a play for you. I love you," she said firmly. "I'm not making any demands on you."

"The hell you're not. It starts with words of love, then ends up demanding everything a man has. I told you there was nothing but physical attraction between us. Don't try to glorify it, Maggie. If you can't handle it, just say so, but don't wrap it up in pretty words to assuage your conscience."

He stood up, dumping her on her feet, waiting only until she had her balance before releasing her to pace across the room. He turned and glared at her. "I don't buy it."

"What?" Suddenly conscious of her state of undress, Maggie looked around for her shirt. She snatched it up from the floor and shrugged into it, fastening the buttons to gain a modicum of modesty. Her heart hurt, it pounded so hard. She felt a bit sick. Dragging her fingers through her hair to try for some semblance of normalcy, she faced him again. He looked like the Viking warrior she'd first imagined. His hair shone gold in the lamplight. His stance, fists on hips, legs widespread and planted, reminded her even more of the warrior image. Anger radiated from him. How could three small words have wrought such a change?

"I don't buy this bit about your *love*. When I got home tonight, you were flirting with Lance and every other cowboy on the ranch. Now after a few wild kisses, you say you're in love with me. Not in this lifetime, sweetheart. Maybe you like the idea of me taking care of you for the rest of your life. And finding out our kisses aren't too hard to handle, you decide to make your play."

"Stop it! It's not like that at all! You were the one suggesting we practice because I don't have much experience. Even tonight, you made me write down what I felt. This started out as nothing but a lesson from you."

"Right, for the affair you agreed to have. But at the end of your stay, you leave, no regrets, no strings."

"I didn't plan to fall in love with you!"

"But how convenient that you did," he said sardonically.

"Stop sneering, it isn't becoming. Forget what I said. You're right, of course. I would be a fool to fall in love with you. You don't have any love left to give anyone.

You'd rather wallow in the fact Jeannie turned out to be different from what you wanted her to be. You'd rather cast every other woman who comes your way in the same light.''

She tossed her head, wanting to claw at the pain in her chest. It wasn't fair. She'd waited for love for so long and when she finally found it, he didn't believe her. And he couldn't love her in return.

"Nice try," he commented, raking her with his hot eyes.

She shrugged, reached for her discarded bra and stuffed it in her pocket. "Think what you want, you will anyway. But I'm not hanging around." Walking across the room proved to be one of the hardest things Maggie had ever done. But she didn't falter, didn't waver. She would wait for the safety and privacy of her room to fall apart. She would not give this arrogant, snide, dumb cowboy the satisfaction of knowing he had hurt her with his scathing words.

Kyle watched her walk out of the room. Heard her footsteps on the stairs, the soft click of her door closing. He couldn't move. Emotions dark and dangerous churned around inside him. How dare she try to convince him she loved him! Damn, did she take him for a tool?

He wanted a drink. As he left the office, he stopped, cocked his head. What was that sound? Closing his eyes, he clenched his fists. *She was crying.* Had she confused passion with love? Had she mixed up the intimacies they'd shared with something more? Did she really believe what she'd said, or was she just another lying schemer, like Jeannie, now distraught because her plan had gone awry?

He stormed into the kitchen, searching for the bourbon he kept in the cabinet near the refrigerator. Pouring himself a tall drink, he leaned against the counter and crossed his arms over his bare chest. Something wound tightly inside him as he sipped the liquor.

He never should have let her stay. He knew she wasn't right for the job, but they'd been without anyone to do the cooking for so long he'd relented. He should have sent her packing that first day. Or at least after she had made a mess of the first two meals. Or when she'd forgotten to dry his laundry. Or the first time he'd kissed her.

God, mistake number two, kissing her. Offering to help with her book. Was he a total idiot, or had he truly thought they could enjoy themselves and then walk away unscathed?

Ten minutes ago he had been ready to make love to her. He still wanted to. He could feel the touch of her satiny skin linger on his fingers. His lips wanted to crush hers beneath his again and kiss her all night long.

Maybe he couldn't blame her for thinking she was falling in love. He'd come on strong and she was innocent and inexperienced. She had confused passion and lust with something more. He'd stay away from her. Keep their relationship strictly business from now on. And first thing in the morning he planned to call the agency and request another housekeeper. He'd keep Maggie until a replacement could be found.

Satisfied things would return to normal, Kyle drained the glass, rinsed it out and left for bed. It had been a day he didn't want to repeat anytime soon.

Passing Maggie's door, he paused a moment, straining to hear anything. There was only silence. He wanted to knock and make sure she was all right. But hesitated. Would she misconstrue that gesture? Probably. He moved down the hall to his own room and closed the door, trying to close out the memory of her soft words of love.

*　　*　　*

Maggie cooked a huge batch of scrambled eggs and bacon. She had toast popping every couple of minutes and the orange juice had been poured at each place. Furious that she'd given in to tears last night, she was extremely conscious of her red swollen eyes. She wanted to have everything ready before anyone came in. She'd leave it all on the table and escape until they'd finished eating. She had tried washing her face with cold water, but the evidence of her crying was blatant.

With a nervous eye on the clock, she willed the eggs to cook faster. She only had a few more minutes before Jack and Billy and the others would troop in. Before Kyle would come from the hall. He was the primary one she wanted to avoid. She felt sick with embarrassment at her naive confession last night. How dumb did he think her? No, he didn't think she was dumb, only manipulative and money-hungry and scheming.

She stirred the bubbling eggs. Buttering another batch of toast, she slipped four more slices of bread into the big toaster. Coffee brewed in the big urn. A quick glance around assured her she had everything ready. Once the eggs were done—

"Good morning." Kyle's low voice came from the doorway.

"Good morning," she replied, her gaze firmly on the pan. She certainly wasn't going to run away just because he showed up.

She heard his step as he crossed to the stove and poured himself a cup of coffee. He didn't move away, but she refused to glance at him. She concentrated on the eggs, they were almost finished. She strained to hear any sound from the yard, but the men still hadn't started for the house.

"Maggie, about last night—"

"Excuse me, I need that platter." She carried the heavy pan over to the platter she had warmed. Scraping the eggs onto it, she placed it in the center of the table and risked a glance at the clock. The toaster popped up and she buttered the slices, adding them to the stack she had kept warm in the oven. Outside, she could hear the murmur of voices.

"Maggie," Kyle said.

She put the toast on the table, checked that everything was there, then scooted around Kyle and headed for the hallway.

"Where are you going?"

"I've eaten," she lied, hurrying to escape before he could stop her. She almost ran to her room, closing the door and leaning against it. There, she'd done it. The first hurdle, their first meeting after last night. She hadn't handled it as calmly as she would have liked, but it was the best she could do.

The knock came suddenly and unexpected.

"Open the door, Maggie."

"Go away." She pushed away and crossed to the window. What did he want from her, blood?

Kyle turned the knob and pushed the door open, hesitating in the opening.

"Maggie, I want to talk to you."

"There's nothing to talk about. Go eat your breakfast."

"Did you really eat?"

"I'll get something later. You better get it now, while it's hot," she said, fiddling with the curtain.

She heard his steps cross her room and tensed. She was not surprised when he put his hand on her shoulder and gently turned her around. His finger beneath her chin raised it until she looked at him.

It hurt. She loved him, had just discovered it, and he didn't believe her. He thought she thought like Jeannie, wanting him for his money.

"I'm sorry for the tears," Kyle said softly.

"Kyle, if you have something to say, say it, then get out. I don't need any false sympathy," she said, anger starting to build. So she made a fool of herself. Only her pride was really damaged. She didn't regret loving him, only that she had voiced her feelings.

"Last night things got out of hand. We were supposed to be doing research for your book."

She nodded. What a joke that turned out to be. Her book was the farthest thing from her mind right now. She wished he would stop touching her. She couldn't think when he touched her.

"So maybe feelings got exaggerated," he continued.

She nodded. *Just leave.*

He sighed. "I'm not making things any better, am I?"

She shook her head.

"Come down to breakfast."

"No. I'll eat when you go out to work." She stepped back, breaking contact, able to breathe again.

Kyle started to say something, thought better of it, and turned to leave.

Maggie followed his progress from the sound of his steps. Taking a deep breath, she turned to gaze out the window. Even now she had hoped he would say something to show he wasn't totally indifferent to her. And he hadn't. As soon as the men left, she'd call the agency and ask Mrs. Montgomery to send a replacement as soon as she found one.

It was after nine by the time Kyle finally left the house. Maggie was starving. She'd been up most of the night, and only nibbled a couple pieces of bacon while she'd prepared breakfast. She went to the kitchen, stacked the dirty dishes and ran water in the sink. Quickly she prepared herself a small omelet. But once it sat on her plate, she toyed with the food. She wished she could turn the clock back to yesterday, do things differently. For one thing, she would never have admitted falling in love. And knowing now what she should have known then, she would not have permitted Kyle to kiss her. How had she ever thought she would be able to walk away unscathed after such mind-boggling kisses? After the first one she should have run far and fast.

Once the kitchen was straight, she went to the office to call Mrs. Montgomery.

"Hello, dear. Are you calling about a new position?" Mrs. Montgomery asked once Maggie had identified herself.

"Yes, I guess I am. Also, I wanted you to look for another housekeeper for the Rafter C."

"Mr. Carstairs already called that order in earlier this morning. I'm searching, but as I told you when I referred you to the place, he's not an easy man to please. I was surprised he said you could stay until a replacement could be found."

Kyle had already called to have her replaced. The knowledge pierced her. She tried to keep her voice level, all the while wanting to slam down the receiver and scream in anger. He couldn't wait for her to write her book and leave, he had taken steps to find her replacement as soon as possible.

". . . anything earlier, do you still wish to leave before I find a replacement for the ranch?" Mrs. Montgomery said.

"What? Yes, I want to leave if you find anything else for me." She would not stay a day longer than she needed to. But for the time being, she needed the money. And a place to stay.

"Very well, Miss Foster, I'll call if I find anything suitable."

Maggie had to be satisfied with that. She knew Mrs. Montgomery didn't think highly of her work skills. And the woman was right. But it was time to show her she could do a job.

Turning to her computer, she sat down to work. She wasn't going to worry about doing the job at the Rafter C to Kyle's exacting standards. He'd already made his decision. He didn't want her here. He could have at least let her be the one to leave.

Reading about the characters she had conceived, she soon lost sight of the problems that plagued her. She had to get them going so she could finish the book and send it off.

When the phone rang, Maggie glanced up. It was time to take a break, she'd been at it all morning. Glancing at the clock, she froze. Past time to prepare lunch. She saved her work and reached for the phone.

Maggie flew into the kitchen a few minutes later. It was almost time for the men to come in and she hadn't started lunch. The call from Kyle's sister had taken far longer than she had expected. Now she scrambled around to cut the ham and roast beef, slather mayonnaise on the bread. She heard the horses and the voices. Hurrying, she made them each one. She could fix the second round while they ate the first. In seconds she had enough to start and smiled brightly when they began filtering in.

"Missed you at breakfast," Billy said easily, scanning her up and down as he liked to do to tease.

"I ate early. I'll have more sandwiches ready in only a few minutes. Help yourselves to the tea and coffee." She turned back to the counter, began the process all over again.

Kyle walked in and sat down without saying a word. He began to eat.

Ignoring him was easy with the other men present and Maggie began to relax. She joked with Billy and Jack, filled up their plates again and again and made sure everyone had enough to eat. She refused to sit in the chair beside Kyle, and since there was no other available, she kept busy running back and forth so no one commented on the fact.

"Slow down, girl, you're going to knock yourself out," Lance drawled at one point, flicking his gaze back and forth between Maggie and Kyle.

"I'm fine. Just a bit behind."

"Daydreaming again?" Kyle asked in an obvious bad mood.

"Actually I got held up by a call from your sister. She said to tell you she and her husband are coming for a few days and you're to be nice to Jake," Maggie replied primly, refilling Lance's ice tea.

"You'll like Angel, she's stayed here before and always pitches in," Lance said with a smile.

"She sounded nice on the phone."

Maggie looked just to the left of Kyle. "Which room should I prepare for them?"

"The one across from you. Angel can help with the meals while she's here."

"I got the impression from her call that she and Jake are looking forward to riding a lot."

"Can you manage two more for meals?"

She shrugged and opened another bag of chips and handed them to Pete. "I'm sure I can manage." For as long as I stay, she wanted to add. How she hoped Mrs. Montgomery found something for her before she found a replacement housekeeper. She'd give anything to leave before Kyle asked.

Lunch seemed to last forever. If she even glanced Kyle's way, she saw his gaze on her. She tried to listen to the banter between the cowboys, wistfully remembering a time when it had all been new and exciting. Now she wanted to leave before she made a bigger fool of herself over the suspicious owner of the ranch. She

wanted to turn her back on the Rafter C and any promise
she had once imagined and find another place where she
would keep to herself, do her job and find relaxation in
her writing. She should have learned from Don, but Kyle
had completed the lesson.

Love and marriage and happy-ever-after were only true
in books. She'd not forget that in the future.

CHAPTER NINE

MAGGIE saved another chapter when Kyle walked into the office late that afternoon. She glanced up guiltily and checked the time. Good grief, she should have started dinner a half hour ago. Rising in panic, she shoved in her chair and turned to leave.

"Letter for you." Kyle moved behind his desk and sat down, tossing an envelope across the wide expanse.

Maggie hesitated, puzzled. "No one knows where I am," she murmured, crossing to the desk. Her old address had been crossed out and Kyle's ranch address penciled in by the post office. Her heart sank, the letter was from her father.

"Thanks." She picked it up and slid it into her back pocket. She would have to read it, but later, after dinner. Turning, she hurried to the kitchen. She had been planning a meat loaf for dinner, but there wasn't time, now, to prepare it. It would have to be hamburgers. At least Kyle wouldn't suspect she'd forgotten about the meal. She could have everything ready when the men came in. If she didn't, she wouldn't be surprised to find Kyle would fire her outright, instead of waiting until the Montgomery Agency found a replacement.

Dinner proved to be strained. Maggie did her best to appear carefree and unconcerned, but every instinct was trained on Kyle. He ate, took no part in the general conversation, and his attitude caused comment from his men.

As soon as he finished eating, he left for the office. One or two raised eyebrows were all that the cowboys allowed, but she knew everyone was curious about the reason for Kyle's attitude.

She washed the dishes. Then, instead of heading back to the office to work on her book, she went out front and walked slowly down the long driveway. The early evening air was still balmy and the breeze that blew from the west carried a hint of the coolness from the snow-capped mountains. It was pleasant and she felt a certain peace seep through her.

Now was as good a time as any to read the letter from her father. She pulled it from her back pocket, feeling the tension rise just seeing his dark, bold letters. His handwriting reminded her of Kyle. They were two of a kind, domineering and autocratic. Why did they feel they had the right to run their own lives and the lives of those they touched?

She slid her finger beneath the envelope flap and withdrew the two pages within. He demanded she return home, forget her foolishness and settle down. He wanted to know where she was, why the phone had been disconnected. He ended saying Don had asked after her and if she were at all smart she'd snap up such a fine man.

Rereading the letter, Maggie searched for any indication that her father wanted to know her feelings in the matter, to find a trace of concern for her own desires and plans for the future. There were none. It was a demand for return, clear and simple.

She sighed and tucked the letter back into the envelope and slid it back into her pocket. Nothing had changed. Not that she had expected it to change, but she always hoped that just once her father would ask about her and then listen to what she had to say. Listen and respect her own views, her own feelings, her own desires.

By the time Maggie reached the main highway, it had grown dark. She recognized the main road with a start of surprise. She had been daydreaming, again, and hadn't realized how far she'd walked. It was two miles back to the house. And it would be pitch dark before she covered half the distance. There were no streetlights, no traffic to provide some illumination. She would be lucky to stay on the blacktop and not wander off into the barbed-wire fencing.

With a shake of disgust, she turned and walked quickly back the way she'd come. How could she have let herself get caught up in daydreams again? She really needed to get a better grasp of reality. Save her daydreaming for when she sat before the computer and composed her story.

In only seconds she saw headlights. Then the truck pulled up beside her and Kyle's angry face looked out from the window.

"What the hell are you doing here? Can't you see it's almost dark!"

"Yes." Calmly she tossed her head and kept walking. She'd rather run into the barbed-wire fence than deal with him.

"Get in, I'll take you back."

"No, thanks." She could still see the road, and if she walked in the center couldn't she—

"Maggie, get into the truck before I get out and put you in." The angry voice brooked no refusal.

She hesitated a second, long enough to assuage her pride, then conceded. She didn't want to walk all the way back in total darkness.

Once inside, Kyle turned the truck around on the narrow road and roared toward the house.

"Bad news in your letter?" he asked.

Maggie ignored his comment. She wanted to tell him it was none of his business. How would he feel if she parroted his words to him?

"Maggie!"

"No bad news. Just the usual stuff from my father. He wants to dictate my life and I refuse. I don't know why he persists." Except he thought it his given right to dictate her life. When would he get it through his head she was grown and on her own? And perfectly capable of running her own life. Well, she qualified honestly, maybe not perfectly capable or she wouldn't be in the fix she found herself now. But it was her life and her mistakes and she didn't want anyone interfering.

"He doesn't know where you are, does he? My address was added from the post office."

"I didn't tell him where I was going. Not that it is any of your business," she said tartly.

"Call him, Maggie. Tell him you're here and give him the address and phone number. You owe him that much."

"I don't believe you have any more right to dictate my life than my father does. Less, actually. Butt out, Kyle," she said, turning in the dark cab and glaring at him. She wished he could see her.

"I'm not dictating your life, I'm only telling you to call the man, let him know where you are." It was a reasonable response. Why was she trying to make more of it than what it was? Was she looking for a fight? For a moment Kyle was ready to offer her one.

"I'll take it under consideration," she said through gritted teeth. If that wasn't an order, she didn't know what was.

"Call him tonight."

"I believe I know how to run my own life."

"I don't think you have a clue," Kyle snapped as he jerked the pickup to a stop and killed the engine.

"I certainly do. I'm managing just fine."

"From where I'm, sitting, it doesn't look like it." He reached across the bench seat and latched his hands onto her upper arms, dragging her across until she practically sat in his lap. He lowered his face until he could see hers in the dim light spilling from the kitchen window.

"Maggie, you can't stay here. I've already called Mrs. Montgomery and asked for a new housekeeper."

"I know. I called her myself to suggest it and she told me you'd beaten me to it. I'll be going soon."

"And just what are you going to do? You didn't make it in the office job, nor the store, nor the fast food, nor here."

Damn, had Mrs. Montgomery shared all that with him? It was none of his business. She shrugged, trying to escape his hands, but he only tightened his grip. "I know, I know, but I'm doing better as a housekeeper. I'll look for another position like it. Don't you worry about it. Maybe I didn't suit you, but I'll suit some other family, and still have time to write my book. If I can just get it published, I'll have enough money to live on until I write a second. That's what I really want to do."

He remained silent for a long moment, surprised at the anger that churned up at her declaration she'd find another housekeeper job. He didn't want her cooking for some other man. He didn't want some randy rancher teaching her how to kiss and helping her do research for her blasted book. Yet she couldn't stay. She imagined herself in love with him. There was nothing he could do but send her away before she became a nuisance.

When he fell in love, he wanted a woman like his mother. Someone who kept the house immaculate, cooked delicious, bountiful meals, and had time to take care of any children they might have. He didn't want some flighty, scatterbrained woman who daydreamed most of her life away, who couldn't cook beyond basics, and who thought nothing of flirting with the cowhands.

Yet as she stared at him so defiantly in the faint light, his heart turned over. She was so pretty, her eyes wide and luminous, her hair softly swirling around her shoulders, her lips tempting. He drew in a deep breath and took in her own special scent, evening air, roses, and Maggie.

He wanted to thrust her away from him and order her to call her father. Maybe the man could get her to go home and then take care of her. But his arms didn't work that way, they were drawing her closer. His mouth didn't voice the thoughts that he knew he should say, instead it covered hers and kissed her long and deep.

When her hands clenched against his shirt, bunching it beneath her fingers, and pulled him closer, something inside relaxed and he drew her fully into his arms. She represented sweetness and innocence, allure and desire all wrapped up into one enticing little package. And for the moment, that was all he wanted.

"Go home, Maggie," he said softly, breaking off the kiss.

Her hands pushed to be released and she slid across the seat to the passenger door. Opening, she blinked in the light from the overhead bulb. "When you have a replacement or I find another job. Until then, I work here!" She stepped out, slammed the door and stalked to the house, the blood racing through her veins at his embrace. Torn between anger and desire, she stomped up the three wooden steps and marched through the kitchen, intent on resuming her writing. She hated Kyle telling her what to do. And she didn't admire his methods one bit. Did he think he could kiss her into submission, bend her to his will through his lips? She was made of sterner stuff than that.

He was just as demanding as her father and she couldn't believe she had thought for a single moment that she loved him. The emotions churning around inside right now didn't resemble love at all. She was mad enough to spit nails! How dare he think he could seduce her to his will. She'd show him. She would not call her father. She would not leave until she was good and ready to go.

Tomorrow, she would send what she had written to a publisher. There was enough now for a publisher to get a good idea of what she'd done so far, and where she was heading.

She closed the office door behind her, hoping it would clearly indicate to Kyle that she wanted to be alone. It didn't work. By the time she had found her place on the most recent chapter, he opened the door, and strode to his desk.

She heard the creak of his chair, but kept her eyes resolutely on the monitor. She would not be swayed by his presence. He'd made his feelings abundantly clear. He wanted her gone. He had no use for any love from her or anyone else, as far as she could tell.

Trying to concentrate on the story line was impossible. Excruciatingly aware of Kyle, she heard the scratch of the pen across paper, the rustle as he turned pages, the squeak in his chair as he shifted position. She knew he frowned as he read some of the reports, his soft breathing resonated in the quiet room. Longing to look at him, just once, she denied herself that pleasure. She was here to write, and that she would do if it killed her!

Slowly she typed in a few words. She wasn't even sure what she was doing, but she would not let him know that. She typed in more. She would have to read it all tomorrow and see if there was anything she could keep, or if it were total gibberish. But for now she would look as if she were working and hadn't a care in the world.

Tension filled the room, shimmered between them, grew. Maggie felt as if her nerves were stretched so taut they might pop. She stared at the screen, trying to figure out what the words said, but every aspect of her body focused on the sounds from Kyle's desk. It couldn't hurt just to glance over and see what he was doing.

Slowly she moved her head, her eyes.

He stared right back at her.

Her gaze locked with his and heat rose in her cheeks. She couldn't look away. The anger fled and hurt took its place. She loved him, everything about him. From his bossy, demanding ways, to the way his skin crinkled around his eyes. From the arrogant, stubborn jut of his jaw, to the soft way he threaded his fingers into her hair when he kissed her. From the strength he displayed to his men, to the friendship he had offered when helping her with her book. Why couldn't he have returned just some of that affection? Why couldn't he have let her stay to explore the attraction between them, see if love could grow on his part as it had on hers?

Kyle muttered something, threw down his pen and stormed from the room. Maggie leaned back in her chair, exhausted. Sadly she pressed the keys to save the chapter and turned off her computer. She'd take a bath and go to bed. Tomorrow she'd mail off what she'd written and keep her fingers crossed.

For the next two days Maggie avoided Kyle. Except for meals, they rarely caught a glimpse of each other. She considered moving her computer to her bedroom, but Kyle seemed to be avoiding the office, and she began to relax enough to write. She drove into Cheyenne, bought some more groceries and mailed her first six chapters off. Stopping in at the Montgomery Agency, she told Mrs. Montgomery she wanted another housekeeping job. Apparently Kyle had not told the woman the full extent of Maggie's lack, and the woman promised she'd look for a similar position.

Maggie hadn't called her father, but she wrote him a short note and mailed it from Cheyenne. In it she explained she had found a job working on a ranch and was doing fine. She gave no return address, however. She would be at the Rafter C for such a short time, no sense worrying her father with multiple addresses. When she got her next job, she'd send him her address.

It was midafternoon on the third day after Maggie had sent in her chapters when she heard a car. She'd had so much energy that morning, she'd cleaned the house from top to bottom and done two loads of laundry. A savoury stew simmered on the stove and she planned to make homemade bread for dinner. A chocolate cake waited to be frosted.

She glanced out the window, curious to see if it were Kyle's sister and her husband. They were due today.

The big Jeep stopped near the back door and in only a few moments, a tall, blond woman entered the kitchen, followed by an even taller dark-haired man. Both were in jeans and shirts and looked relaxed and happy.

"Hi, you must be Maggie. I'm Angelica Morgan." Kyle's sister was friendly and easy to like. She shook hands with Maggie and introduced her husband, Jake.

Maggie greeted him, feeling his intense interest as he shook hands. He was the cop, and she knew instantly he must be a good one. His entire attention focused on her for a brief time. He stood even taller than Kyle, and was very good-looking, in a rough, dark way. From the way Angelica watched him, love so clearly evident in her eyes, Maggie knew his wife adored him.

Feeling a bit awkward acting as hostess in Angelica's childhood home, Maggie offered them drinks.

"We want to get some riding in before dinner. Where shall we dump our stuff?" Angelica asked once they had ice tea.

"Top of the stairs, to the left."

"Good, my room as a child. Come on, Jake, I'll show you where I ran to escape Kyle's bossy ways."

With a bright smile to Maggie, Angelica led the way to her room, Jake following with two small bags.

So, Maggie thought as she frosted the cake, she wasn't the only one to find Kyle bossy. She smiled, remembering his mentioning one time he had tried to keep Jake away from Angelica. He was as bad as her father in some respects, but obviously he didn't have the ability to make Angelica do what he wanted, anymore than her father had.

And in all fairness, Kyle listened to her on many things. Wasn't the ranch enough to run? Did he have to try to run other's lives, as well?

The next morning Angelica invited Maggie to accompany them riding.

"Come ride with us. Kyle's showing us the new dam and the pond that resulted. It'll be fun. We can make up sandwiches and eat lunch out on the range. You have to make sandwiches for the men anyway."

"I don't know, there's a lot to do around here."

"Tell her to come with us, Kyle. It'll do her good to see more of the ranch," Angelica entreated her brother.

He looked at Maggie, his expression carefully neutral. "Come if you wish."

She hesitated. She felt as if she had been cooped up in the house for days. She had taken walks each afternoon to get out of the house, but done nothing strenuous or exciting. And it would be exciting to spend the day with Kyle, no matter how little he wanted her. She could save up memories to take out in future years, see more of his home, and always remember him as the tall, golden warrior of her fantasies. Would she ever meet another man who would capture her fancy so strongly?

"Okay. Let me get lunches for everyone, then I'll be ready," Maggie capitulated.

"I'll help," Angelica said, already turning to the refrigerator.

"Come on, Jake, you can help me saddle the horses," Kyle said unexpectedly.

"Kyle—" Angelica began. Jake reached out and clasped the nape of her neck in one hand and drew her up to him.

"Don't worry, Angel. If your big brother gets rough with me, I'll arrest him and haul him off to jail." He lowered his face to kiss her and Maggie watched with wide-eyed envy. Involuntarily her gaze moved to Kyle. He stared at her, his own gaze dropping to her lips as if remembering the kisses they'd shared.

When the lunches were made, Maggie hurried upstairs to don her boots and hat. She glanced at herself in the mirror, satisfied she looked like the others. She knew she could ride well enough to keep up. And soon she'd have more memories to store up for the endless time she was gone. Kyle didn't want her, he'd made that perfectly clear. But it didn't stop the longing in her. Maybe once she moved away from the Rafter C she could begin to forget him, forge a new life away from a man who refused to love her.

The ride proved exhilarating. They alternated loping across the fields and walking to rest the horses and chat. Jake stayed near Angelica, leaving Kyle and Maggie paired up. She kept her horse a reasonable distance away, avoiding any temptation to make the day memorable. It was enough to be with him, to enjoy the bright sunshine, the open spaces and the grass-scented breeze.

Kyle had dammed a small stream where it widened in a draw. There were several huge old cottonwoods near the upper end of the pond and they decided to picnic in the shade. The horses grazed nearby. Spreading out on the blanket Angelica had brought, all four of them soon finished lunch.

Kyle stretched out and covered his face with his hat. "I'm tired," he said.

"I'm not," his sister said, springing up. Holding out her hand to Jake, she smiled at him. "Come on, we'll go exploring."

"Where?" Kyle asked, not bothering to look up.

"Just around. I want to walk the perimeter of the pond. Want to come, Maggie?"

She shook her head. It didn't take genius to know when she would have been a fifth wheel. She watched the couple walk away, Jake's head already bent near Angelica's to hear what she said. Maggie tried to imprint the scene on her mind. It would be perfect in her book and she could make sure the hero—

"We're not a pair. You could have gone with them. I meant it when I said I was tired. I want to take a nap."

"Take it. Don't worry about me," she replied, stretching out her legs. Full from lunch, warmed by the sun, Maggie felt content. She should work something like this into her book, where the heroine is so sated she felt like a satisfied cat. She could curl up in the sun, close her eyes and dream.

Maggie brushed the pesky fly away from her jaw and mumbled something, turning her face away. The tickle came again. Her fingertips brushed her skin. Why wouldn't it go away? She shifted. The ground was hard, the sun still warm and the air gentle as it blew across the Wyoming range.

The fly came back. She brushed it away, rolled over onto her side and pulled her hat across her face. The tickle came back. Snapping open her eyes, she stared right into Kyle's amused gray ones. He dangled a blade of grass against her jaw, tickling, teasing.

She reached up for it, tangling, instead, her fingers with his.

"If you sleep too long now, you won't sleep tonight," he murmured, bringing her fingertips to his lips. Hesitating a long moment, he then kissed them.

"Where are Angelica and Jake?" If she said nothing about his lips against her fingers, maybe he'd continue kissing her.

"Still on their walk. I suspect they stopped off for a while."

She lay still, her heart beating slowly as she let her mind imagine the newlyweds stopping for some kissing. She smiled, envious of their happiness. And Kyle leaned over and kissed her.

Shifting onto her back, Maggie reached up to pull him down on top of her, his chest almost crushing her beneath his weight. His tongue made sweet forays into her mouth, his hands threaded in her hair and massaged her scalp. Even though she had not been sleeping well at night, she would gladly forgo a nap this afternoon for kisses like this.

Far too soon for Maggie, Kyle sat up and pulled her to a sitting position. "They are coming back," he said, rising and heading for the horses.

Maggie drew her fingers through her hair, trying for some order, then slapped her hat on. She hadn't questioned the interlude, but now she began to wonder. Why had he kissed her? They had not spoken for days, suddenly he acted as if he wanted her again. Or was it just that he wanted somebody since Angelica and Jake were paired? Confused, Maggie began to pack away the debris from the picnic and had almost cleared the blanket by the time Angelica and Jake appeared.

"Sorry we took so long," Angelica said, reaching out to help Maggie fold the blanket.

"Not a problem. I took a short nap. It's nice to doze in the sun."

Angelica looked at her sharply, then at her brother as he brought two of the horses over. Jake followed with the other two. "It sure can be."

They rode over more of the range, Kyle and Angelica commenting on the changes Kyle had made, things that remained the same year after year. Jake and Maggie were along for the ride and to learn more about the ranch, but had little to contribute to the conversation.

When they reached home, Kyle had one of the ranch hands unsaddle the horses. Maggie cleaned up then went back downstairs to start dinner. She hoped spaghetti would be fine. Angelica joined her in only a few moments and began to butter the garlic bread.

Dinner preparation was well under way when Kyle came into the kitchen. He glanced at Jake in the middle of cutting up fresh vegetables for a salad, his sister helping. But it was to Maggie he looked. Holding out another forwarded envelope, he glared down at her.

"This came today. I thought I told you days ago to call your father. This is the second letter you've received from him forwarded because he doesn't have a clue where you are."

"You told me," she returned.

"You didn't call him?"

"No, and I'm not calling him tonight, either, so forget throwing your weight around."

"Then give me his number and I'll call him. The man's probably frantic to know where you are."

"I will not. My father has been running my life for long enough. I'm in charge now and I will contact him how and when I wish. You stay out of it."

"Call him now," Kyle said.

"No!"

"As your boss, I'm ordering you to call him tonight."

She stared at him, aware Jake and Angelica had stopped working and were staring at them both. Slowly she shook her head.

"I'm serious, Maggie."

"So am I. Stay out of my business."

"I'll find the number. He lives in Colorado Springs, according to the address on the letter."

She snatched the letter away and held it behind her back. "Leave it alone, Kyle. It's not your business."

"While you work here, it is."

"Then I'll leave immediately."

In the silence the soft bubbling of the spaghetti water was loud. The hum of the refrigerator grew as she stared at him. She took a deep breath. She refused to allow him to interfere, to dictate to her. She had already had a lifetime of that.

Kyle stared at her for another moment, then closed his eyes and dragged his fingers through his hair. Turning, he headed out of the room. "Don't leave until you get another job," he said.

Maggie glanced over at Angelica and Jake. Their eyes were focused on the salad preparations, but Maggie knew they had heard every word. Her own curiosity would have been in overdrive. Shakily, she smiled. "I have a thing about being bossed around. Kyle seems to bring out the worst in me," she said.

Angelica met her eyes and nodded sympathetically. "I know, but he usually means it for the best."

Maggie nodded. "Maybe. But whose best, mine or his?" She folded the envelope and stuffed it inside her pocket. Another letter from her father, and another confrontation with Kyle. Maybe she should call Mrs. Montgomery in the morning and see if she had found anything promising. She didn't know how long she could stay on the Rafter C.

Maggie headed for the office after doing the dishes. She hadn't seen Kyle or the Morgans since dinner ended. She hoped they were watching television or had gone for a walk. But as she approached the office door, she heard them. Sighing with the lost opportunity to work on her book, she almost turned away when she heard her name.

"Maggie's not your sister. It was bad enough when you tried to boss me around all the time. She's just an employee."

"Get off my back, Angel." Kyle's voice was hard.

"Or maybe she's more than an employee," Angelica suggested.

"No."

"You watch her all the time. I don't remember you watching Rachel."

"I don't watch her all the time. Sometimes I look at her but, hell, she's pretty, easy on the eyes. The men look at her, too."

"There's more to it than that. I know you two were kissing at the picnic. Her lips were swollen and rosy when we got back."

"Jake, take your wife out and distract her," Kyle said.

Maggie heard Jake's low chuckle. "Come on, Angel. You've said enough."

"No, not yet. Kyle, you're going to drive her away with this kind of attitude."

"She's leaving soon anyway." There was no emotion in his tone.

"Why? She's great for the place. She cooks good food, keeps the house clean. And as you say, she's easy on the eye. Why get rid of her?"

"She's nothing like Mom, for one thing."

"What does that have to do with anything?" Angel's voice was clearly perplexed.

"If you're trying to play matchmaker, you should know I don't think she'd fit in. She's much more like Jeannie than Mom."

"She's nothing like Jeannie. And if you think so, you better take a course in interpersonal skills."

"Spoken like a true college professor."

"Ease up on her, Kyle. You're her employer, not her father, or her keeper."

Maggie knew she should leave. It was wrong to eavesdrop. Yet she couldn't move, fascinated by the trend of the conversation. She crept closer until she could see into the room. The hall was dark, maybe no one would notice her standing there.

Jake leaned back in her chair, half turned from her as he watched his wife. Angelica sat on the edge of the desk, leaning over toward her brother. Suddenly Kyle stood up and walked to the window, his back to the others.

"I know I'm not her keeper. I just think she should let her father know where she is."

"You were practically browbeating her over it."

"I know."

"You can't control her actions, Kyle," Angelica said gently.

"I want to."

"You always want to be in control."

He hesitated a long time, then turned back to his sister. "If I can be in control, maybe bad things won't happen."

Maggie stared at him. The silence in the office stretched out for several long moments as Angel and Jake also stared at Kyle.

"You mean, like your mother and father dying in an automobile accident?" Jake asked at last, understanding coming to him before the others.

Kyle nodded, his eyes on his sister. "That's why I told Jake to stay away from you a couple of years ago. I didn't want you hurt. I wanted to control things so you would always be around and never get hurt.''

''Oh, Kyle.'' Angelica hopped off the desk and went to her brother, hugging him. ''You aren't God. You can't determine if accidents will happen or not. You can't determine who gets hurt and who doesn't. You can't change fate.''

Maggie slipped away, walking softly so no one would hear her. She tiptoed up the stairs and entered her room, closing the door silently behind her. She should not have eavesdropped. Sinking on her bed, she closed her eyes, still seeing Kyle by the window, explaining why he tried so much to be in total control. He was still reacting to the loss of his parents when he'd been a boy. His desire for control had arisen from the belief if he controlled things, nothing bad would happen. Her heart melted. And her arms longed to encircle him as Angelica's had done.

CHAPTER TEN

MAGGIE tried to recall all she knew of Kyle's background. Kyle's bossy behavior resulted from the tragic loss of his parents when he'd been a child. He had hoped to avert anything like it again by controlling everything around him. Probably because nothing as devastating had happened since that accident, he thought the technique worked.

For a long time she wondered if Kyle would always be that way, or if now that he recognized his actions for what they were, he would ease up a bit.

Suddenly Maggie thought of her father and of the way his life had changed when his wife left. Had he been trying to avert another tragedy by controlling everything he could, just like Kyle? Had that been the reason he wanted to control every aspect of her life? To keep her safe and near him. To keep him from experiencing another loss as he had when his wife had left?

For the first time in months, Maggie wanted to talk to her father. She wanted to know if what she suspected was true. If so, they needed to discover if they could have a normal relationship. If he could accept that by the very fact she was his daughter she would always love him, maybe he could relinquish some of his need for control. Loving him didn't mean she had to live her life to his whims. Could he change?

It wasn't late. She could call tonight.

Getting up, she brushed her hair, and raised her chin. Opening her door, she descended the stairs, making a bit more noise than usual to alert those in the office to her presence. But when she reached the door, only Kyle sat behind the desk. The Morgans were gone.

He looked up when she walked in, his eyes dark and shadowed. He didn't speak.

"I thought I would call my father," she said, standing near the door. Would he gloat now that he got his way? She would set him straight if he began—

He nodded and stood. "The phone's there. I'll leave so you'll have some privacy."

He crossed to the door before she stopped him.

"Kyle?"

Turning, he looked at her.

She didn't know what to say. She wanted to tell him what she'd learned, what she guessed about her father, but that would reveal her eavesdropping and she dare not do that. Finally she shrugged and smiled tentatively. "I'll find you when I'm done so you can get back to work."

He nodded and walked out.

With nervous fingers she dialed the familiar number. When her father answered, Maggie took a deep breath. "Hi, Dad, this is Maggie."

Maggie slowly replaced the receiver. Glancing up at the clock on the wall, she was startled to discover how much time she and her father had spent on the phone. But it had been well worth it. They had made tentative steps to close the breach and rediscover the love that existed between them. He would probably always offer his opinion on what she should do, but at least he had admitted being afraid for her, and wanting to protect her from life's harsh realities. She hoped she had convinced him she had to learn some of the realities on her own. They had made a start.

And she owed it to Kyle. She smiled and stood up. She needed to find him and let him know his office was free, if he wanted to return to work. And thank him. He'd think his bossy orders had turned the tide, and she would have to let him think that. She dare not reveal what she'd overheard.

Kyle propped his feet on the wooden railing and tilted his chair back. The night became alive with rustling leaves, distant cattle calls and the stomp of the horses in the corral. His sister and her husband had gone for a walk. Maggie was calling her father. And he sat alone.

For a moment the loneliness he tried to keep at bay swept through him. He thought back to Jeannie and the life together he'd thought they would share. Looking back, he saw clearly that she had never promised him to stay on the ranch and help it grow. She had always been anxious to go into town, to have people visit, to travel. She liked excitement, thrills and fast times. And she had never done a thing around the house.

Of course, he had had Rachel in those days. Would he have discovered more quickly Jeannie's lack of staying power if she had had to do the housework like Maggie? If he had insisted they stay home and develop similar interests?

It didn't matter. She was gone. And he had learned a valuable lesson. When he tried the matrimony stakes again, if he ever tried again, he'd look for a country woman, one who liked ranches and cooking and didn't have different goals. Like writing books.

He shook his head. He couldn't deny the attraction between him and Maggie. He couldn't deny he liked being with her, liked her smile, her wide-eyed wonder at every aspect of ranching. But she couldn't keep her mind on cooking. And everything he had that had once been white now looked a peculiar color of green. He knew she'd mixed something up in the wash.

Maybe he should think of finding someone. Rafe had found Charity. Angel had found Jake. That left him without a partner in the only family he had.

"Kyle?" Maggie peeked out the screen door.

"Finished your call?" How had that gone? "Mend any fences?"

"Yes to both questions." She came out onto the porch and walked slowly to the column holding up the porch roof. Leaning against it, she stared out across the range.

"I'm sure your father was glad to hear from you," Kyle said, watching her in the faint starlight.

"He was worried about me. Now he's not. Where did Angelica and Jake go?"

"For a walk." They had gone off, holding hands, already lost in their own world of love. Kyle shifted restlessly. Watching Maggie increased the yearning for his own mate. Not her, but someone stable and down to earth. Someone like his mother had been.

"You can use your office now. I'm through in there for tonight."

"Not writing?"

"No." She glanced over to where he sat as if she wanted to say something. But she remained silent, only turning and walking back into the house without another word.

Kyle heard the screen door close and knew she'd gone. He was still alone.

The next morning Maggie rose at her regular time and had breakfast well in hand when Angelica joined her.

"I was coming to help," Angelica said after greeting Maggie.

"No need. I've got this part down pat, anyway. Help yourself to coffee," Maggie said cheerfully. Things looked a bit better in the daylight. She couldn't get rid of the ache in her heart about Kyle, but she had to look on the bright side. Her relationship with her father looked to be stronger. Her manuscript was already on its way. She could work on the rest of it while she waited to hear when her last day on the Rafter C would be.

"Kyle was lucky to find you. He's not been real lucky with the housekeepers he's had since Rachel left," Angelica said as she slid into an empty seat and sipped the hot coffee.

"Actually, I already have my marching orders. As soon as he finds a replacement, or I get a new job, I'm gone. I'm only hoping I last longer than the four-weeks person. Then I'll hold the record," Maggie said lightly, belying the ache in her heart.

Angelica slammed down her cup and stared at Maggie. "Are you saying Kyle doesn't want you here?"

Maggie shook her head, then nodded. "I am saying that, and no, he doesn't want me here." It hurt to say the words, and Maggie longed to change the subject.

"He's certifiably nuts. Why?"

Because I was foolish enough to fall in love with him, Maggie thought. She smiled gamely and shrugged. "I'm not the world's best housekeeper. I forget to start the meals, I burn them sometimes. I did his laundry once and forgot to dry it and the next day he didn't have anything to wear." Maggie wouldn't mention the time her green shirt had bled on all his white things. Maybe he had never noticed the light green tinge.

"I haven't heard a single complaint since I've been here," Angelica said slowly.

"Probably not. For all my ineptitude, I still beat the men having to fend for themselves. Anyway, Kyle has asked the employment agency for a replacement. As soon as they find one, I'll leave."

"I'd go now," Angelica said darkly. "If he doesn't like what you are doing, let him do it himself."

Maggie stared at Kyle's sister. If she had any pride, she'd probably do that. But she couldn't. If she could stay for a few more days, that would offer a little longer in his presence. She just couldn't leave yet. "Actually, I don't have anything else lined up, so this is a job until I find something."

"And if he gets a replacement first?"

"I'll have to worry about that when the time comes."

Jake wandered in just then and Maggie gratefully changed the subject.

Maggie served up breakfast when the cowboys came in. Placing Angelica beside her brother with Jake on her left, Maggie made room for herself between Lance and Jack. She was the most comfortable with these two men and liked being some distance from Kyle. Not that she could escape his angry glare every time she spoke with Lance. When he saw her laughing at something Lance said, his eyes frosted and he didn't take them from her until she rose to replenish the coffee cups.

Angelica invited Maggie to join them that morning, but Maggie declined. Much as she longed to go with them, she needed to start building a distance between herself and Kyle, not encourage a closeness he didn't want. Somehow she had to find the strength to walk away one day.

The day passed slowly. Maggie cleaned as much as she needed, then sat down to her computer. But the words didn't come. She gazed out the window for hours, thinking about every minute of her time on the Rafter C. And every second spent with Kyle. She knew she should incorporate aspects in her book, but she wasn't capable of revealing her feelings in mere words. Frustrated, she wondered if writing was for her. Maybe she was fooling herself that she had a chance to get a book published, more than one book published. How many people made a career in writing? Very few.

When the phone rang, Maggie answered. She recognized the woman's voice instantly. Gillian.

"Kyle's out right now." Maggie wanted to tell her he was out to her for the rest of her life, but held her tongue.

"Have him give me a call, he knows the number," Gillian responded gaily.

"I'm sure he does," Maggie muttered darkly as she replaced the receiver. "And he probably won't waste a second in returning your call once he gets the message." Would he take Gillian out again? Or worse, invite her over? Maggie set her jaw. If he did, she'd make other plans. There was no way she'd hang around to see him with another woman.

Kyle didn't come in for lunch. Only half the ranch crew were near the house so Maggie didn't have as much to do as normal. She relished the break, joking with the men that had come in, enjoying their banter.

Lance stopped by before he left after lunch. "Everything okay with you?" he asked.

Maggie smiled. "Sure. Why not?"

He shrugged, his eyes studying her. "I don't know. Something's different. You didn't appear to be all there at lunch."

Maggie avoided his eyes. "Most of me was there. I'm trying to figure out the next scene in my book," she replied vaguely. She would not admit to the disturbing thoughts of Kyle and Gillian.

"Want to go into town Friday night? We can go to The Last Roundup, dance a little."

Maggie considered it. She had had fun last time, met friendly neighbors. But she slowly shook her head. "Thanks, Lance. But not this week. Maybe another time?" She was not staying, no need to make friends only to say goodbye in a couple of weeks.

"Sure thing. See you later." Lance raked his fingers through his hair and set his hat on firmly. His boots rang on the wooden floor as he crossed to leave.

For a moment Maggie almost called him back. She remembered how angry Kyle had been when she and Lance had gone out the last time. Even though Kyle had gone out the same night with Gillian. Would another evening spent with Lance evoke a similar response? Or would Kyle shrug his shoulders this time and ignore her? She wished she could evoke some response in him.

She didn't know what she wanted, she thought as she sat again before her computer. She should be concentrating on her future instead of mooning over some cowboy who didn't want her. But it was hard to concentrate on being creative when every fiber of her being longed to be with him. She wanted to watch him work at his desk, watch him interact with his men, watch him ride his big horse. She just plain wanted to be with him.

Laboriously she began to type.

"Where the hell is dinner?" Kyle roared sometime later.

Maggie spun around, staring at him. He stood in the doorway, fists on his hips, glaring at her. He looked hot, dusty and tired. His hat pulled low, his angry stance looked meaner than a sidewinder. Maggie glanced at the clock.

"Ohmygod." She sprang up and crossed the room. It was almost seven and she hadn't even started dinner.

Kyle didn't budge. She stopped inches from him, feeling the anger radiating from him, pouring over her like a wave.

"I forgot."

"You forgot dinner?" His low voice held a note of incredulity.

"I...uh...guess I got caught up in the story and the time just flew by." Maggie shivered at the hard glint in his eyes. Steely with contempt, he stared down at her as if he couldn't believe his eyes, or ears.

"You have fourteen hungry people to feed in less than ten minutes and you forgot to fix the meal?"

"I'll make something." Her mind went blank. What could she fix in ten minutes that would satisfy everyone? She had planned to thaw some meat, and forgotten. There was little choice in the food because it was almost time to go shopping again.

"What?" he snapped.

"I don't know, but I'll come up with something."

"Omelets again?"

"Maybe!" He goaded her and she didn't need that. She was in the wrong, but she had to go start something for dinner, not stay here and trade words. The longer they argued, the later it would be before she could get started on the meal.

Kyle's hands reached out and caught her shoulders.

"I pay you to cook and clean, not sit in front of your computer all day and waste time writing when you should be taking care of this house." His hands gripped tightly.

"I know. I can make omelets in less than ten minutes." Placing her hand on his chest in a placating gesture, she became immediately intrigued by the slow pounding of his heart, the heat from his body, the sculptured muscles beneath her fingertips. She forgot what she was going to say. "I'm sorry." She rubbed her fingers against him unconsciously.

"You're playing with fire, lady," he growled.

"You're hot enough," she replied daringly, meeting the silver glint of his gaze with a bold one of her own.

He frowned. "I had enough of that with Jeannie. Don't play games, Maggie, I'm not up to it anymore. Go in there and find something for dinner."

Heat washed through her. "I'm not playing games." Her hand fisted and she yanked it away from him. Trying to shake off his hands, she found herself drawn even closer, until his heat engulfed her, until all she could see was blazing silver eyes.

She didn't want the kiss. It was hard and punishing, and meant nothing. Not to him, he'd made that clear. But before she could protest, before she could pull away, it changed. He beguiled and entreated until she could no more resist than she could stop breathing. Stepping even closer, she pressed herself against him and returned the kiss.

Suddenly, Kyle thrust her away. "Get dinner," he snapped, and turned to stride down the hall.

Maggie swayed and reached out for the door frame. Her knees were shaky. She drew in a deep breath and headed for the kitchen. She had less than seven minutes to get something on the table. She'd never make it.

When Maggie walked into the kitchen, Angelica smiled in greeting. The place was a hive of activity. Men cut vegetables, Jake beat a large bowl of eggs, Angelica directed another man to start frying potatoes.

"We thought to have omelets, hashbrowns and biscuits," Angelica said.

Déjà vu, Maggie thought. Her first night the cowboys had rallied around to prepare the same meal. Had she come full circle? Would tonight be her last night here?

Feeling foolish for forgetting, and decidedly un-needed in the midst of all the activity, Maggie never-theless reached for the utensils to set the table. No one seemed to mind the work, but that wasn't the point. It was her job to do and she hadn't done it. Kyle had every reason to be furious with her.

A subdued Maggie endured dinner. She tried to join in the conversation, but, ever conscious of Kyle's eyes on her, lost her train of thought more than once and was unable to contribute much. She insisted on clearing everything herself. Thanking everyone for helping, she avoided Kyle. She hoped he would refrain from making some snide comment, and felt her prayers answered when he departed immediately after eating.

Angelica and Jake were heading back for Laramie after dinner. Maggie said her goodbyes, with promises on both sides to keep in touch. Angelica gave Maggie her address and phone number.

"We are looking for a bigger place, but I'll keep in touch. Come visit us in Laramie sometime."

Maggie nodded but knew she would never go. Once she left the Rafter C it would be too hard to keep in touch. A clean break was best.

She went to her room once the kitchen was clean. Standing by her window, she gazed out over the green fields. It was time to move on. She wasn't pulling her weight. Today had proved that. And the heartache wouldn't go away seeing Kyle every day. She'd left the message from Gillian on his desk. Was he talking with her now?

Tomorrow she'd check in with the agency. If there was not another job available, she'd go home. Her dad wanted her to come to visit. She wanted to talk some more with him, see how far they could come in their own relationship.

She'd leave in the morning.

But when morning arrived, Maggie had second thoughts. Granted she had not been the best house-keeper, but she had done some things right. And she would do more before leaving. Once breakfast ended, she prepared stacks of sandwiches for lunch, left them in the refrigerator and headed for town in the blue and white pickup. She'd purchase enough groceries to last them a couple of weeks. Surely Mrs. Montgomery could find a replacement in that time.

The ranch yard was deserted when Maggie returned. She was grateful. She didn't want anything to slow her down. Quickly she unloaded and put away the groceries.

She gathered up Kyle's laundry, stripping his bed, taking his towels. Everything would be cleaned before the end of the day. That would give him enough clothes to wear until her replacement arrived.

Maggie vacuumed and dusted, wiped the kitchen floor and swept the porches back and front. She had bought pizza again, with her own money. But this time she had plenty. Cooking while she continued to work, she tried frantically to get everything done. When she left to-morrow she wanted the house to shine, and the men to remember her kindly.

Late afternoon, a knock came at the front door. It took Maggie a few seconds to figure it out, no one ever used the front door. She hurried to answer it. A florist delivery truck sat in front of the house. A young man held a huge arrangement of flowers.

"Maggie Foster?" he asked, peering around the bouquet.

"Yes?"

"These are for you." He thrust the vase toward her.

Maggie took them with a smile of delight. No one had ever sent her flowers before. Walking into the kitchen, she set the vase on the table. A small envelope peeked up from amongst the leaves.

"To Maggie. We think you're the best! The Men of the Rafter C."

Tears filled her eyes as Maggie pulled out a chair and sat down, as warmth spread through her. She blinked several times and reread the note. The cowboys had sent her flowers! She felt so special, cherished. Maybe she had done an adequate job in their eyes. She tilted her head to the side and gazed at the pretty bouquet. Daisies, carnations, tiger lilies and baby's breath. The colors blended as tears filled her eyes. She hated to leave. She couldn't stay, but this made it even harder to leave.

Why couldn't Kyle have felt the same way? Why couldn't he think she was the best?

Maggie had three pizzas on the table and opened the oven door to put another three into the oven when the men began trooping in that night. Smiling, she hurried over and hugged each man as he arrived.

Their laughter and awkward pats on her back warmed her as much as the bouquet had.

"Got the flowers, huh?" Billy asked, walking around the table, studying the arrangement from every angle. "They look fine."

"They are wonderful!" Maggie said. "I've never had anyone send me flowers before," she added just as Kyle walked in.

He stared at the flowers, at her happy face, then at the satisfied expressions on the faces of his men. Carefully schooling his own expression, he washed his hands at the sink and sat down.

"I have lots of pizza tonight," Maggie said, setting the timer. "Enough for every one of you to have your own, if you can eat that much."

"What's the occasion?" Kyle asked.

Maggie's eyes flew to his. Had he guessed? She tried to smile. "I went to town to do the shopping, thought it might be nice to have pizza again," she said. Pulling out her chair between Lance and Jack, she sat down quickly, avoiding Kyle's pointed glance at the chair to his right.

"So you liked the flowers?" Lance asked after the first pangs of hunger had been satisfied.

"They are wonderful. I feel so special."

"Remember the feeling so you can write it in your book," Kyle said coolly.

Billy looked up. "Are you writing everything about the ranch down in that book? Am I in your book?"

"Sure, you're the bad guy," Jack said without missing a beat.

"No, I'm not writing about the ranch. But sometimes I have trouble getting emotion into the book." She remembered Kyle's kisses, his insistence she write down what she felt. She knew he remembered, as well. Why was he bringing that up now? To forge a bond between them? Ha! In her dreams.

At least the others didn't know. And wouldn't. After tonight, she'd be long gone. Time enough then to see if she could capture her emotions on paper. She'd have heartache and sadness to add to the delights and pleasure of remembered kisses. A well-rounded fount to draw from, she thought sadly.

She turned back to tease Billy about including him in her book but her heart wasn't in it and she counted the minutes until she could be alone.

Maggie folded all the clean clothes, towels and bedding. She still had to make up Kyle's bed. Hurrying up the stairs, she quickly put everything away and turned to make the bed just as Kyle walked in.

"Oh, sorry. I thought I'd have this done already." She pulled the sheet taut.

"I heard you up here and didn't know what you were doing. I can help." He crossed to the other side of the big bed and reached for the sheet. In only moments the bed was made.

Maggie had to get away. The lure of the big bed, of the sexy cowboy standing only a few feet away, tugged at her. She wanted him to cross the distance, sweep her up into his arms and kiss her like she remembered. Holding her breath for a long moment, she slowly released it. He hadn't moved.

"I put your clean clothes in your drawers or in the closets," she murmured as she edged toward the door.

"Thanks."

"I'll see you at breakfast."

"Maggie—"

"Good night." She almost ran down the hall to her room.

Once safely behind the closed door, she wished she hadn't left. It was her last night. She wished they could have spent it together, maybe sitting on the porch or sharing a cup of coffee in the office. Wished she could have enjoyed the tentative friendship that had passed between them at one time. Just for a few more hours.

Shaking her head, she moved to draw the suitcases from beneath her bed.

Maggie watched each man as he ate breakfast. She'd miss them. She had become fond of them all, from Lance with his kindness, to Billy's flirtatious ways, to Jack's calm way of explaining things to her, to Trevor's always asking for seconds. She refused to look at Kyle. There was no need. She had all the memories of him she could handle.

When the men left, she smiled and wished them a good day, knowing she'd be long gone by the time they returned to the house for dinner.

Taking her time, she prepared lunch to leave for them. Then went to unhook her computer. Knowing if anyone saw her they'd immediately suspect something was wrong, she moved her car to the front of the house, out of sight of the yard, the barn and the curious eyes of the men still on the homestead. She carried the keyboard and base out and carefully placed them in the back of her car. The monitor was heavy, and she was afraid she'd drop it, but it, too, made it safely into the back seat. Finally everything was set.

Returning at last for her suitcases, she put them in the trunk. One last walk through the old house to make sure it was in apple pie order and Maggie was ready to leave.

She called the agency.

Mrs. Montgomery told her she still didn't have another position for her, but one applicant looked promising for the position at the Rafter C.

Satisfied Kyle and his men would be looked after soon, Maggie climbed into her car and headed down the long blacktop driveway.

She had left her father's address on Kyle's desk, just in case any mail arrived for her. Once she reached home she would drop the publisher a note, giving her new address so if they needed to get in touch with her they wouldn't trouble Kyle.

Approaching the highway, Maggie noticed the mail truck pulling away from the large mailbox by the gate.

She stopped and got out. She'd just check one last time for any personal mail, then head for Denver.

The thick manila envelope gave her the first clue. It was addressed to her. Slowly she pulled it out and ripped the end off, pulling out the stack of papers.

Her manuscript. She was surprised by the publisher's extremely quick response. The letter fluttered to the ground. She picked it up, scanned it quickly, her heart in her throat.

Slow tears filled her eyes and slid down her cheeks. On top of everything else, the rejection was too much. She sank down beside her car, crying at the loss of so much at once, from her bright future as a novelist to the deep heartache from walking away from the man she loved.

CHAPTER ELEVEN

MAGGIE wiped her cheeks, rubbed the ache in her chest. She felt like a sad soggy mess. Beneath her the ground trembled, she felt the vibrations and wondered why. Then she caught the movement from the corner of her eye. A rider, coming hard and furiously across the open pasture. Headed straight for the fence.

Slowly she pushed herself upright and wiped her face again with the back of her hand, holding her manuscript pages and letter against her breasts.

Kyle drew his sorrel gelding to a halt on the other side of the barbed-wire fence. He dismounted, his eyes on Maggie. Dropping the reins, he took hold of the wooden fence post and vaulted over the five strands of barbed wire. Never taking his eyes from her, he walked across the blacktop, his spurs ringing. The hot sun blazed down on them and Maggie blinked her lids to clear as much of the tears as she could before—

"What are you doing?" he asked as he drew closer. Taking in the packet of papers clenched to her chest and the tears in her eyes, he reached out for her, understanding instant.

"Aw, honey, didn't they want your book?"

His sympathy was more than she could bear. She burst into fresh tears, shook her head and stepped into his welcoming embrace.

Kyle drew her up tightly, his voice murmuring soothingly into her ear. Maggie leaned against him, drawing from his strength. Beneath her cheek she felt the beating of his heart. And for one last moment she felt safe, cherished, loved. And so lonely she thought she would die.

Taking a shaky breath, she breathed in dust and horse and tangy male scent. She wished she could bottle it to take with her. She wished she could bottle Kyle to take with her. Biting her lip, she tried to stop the tears. Time enough later to give way. She had a long drive ahead of her.

"I'm all right," she said, pushing away, wiping her cheeks.

His hands cupped her face and his thumbs brushed away the trail of tears. Her eyelashes were spiky, her face had to be blotchy from crying. Great, what a wonderful last impression to leave. She sniffed, wishing she could have left before he found her.

"What did the letter say?" Kyle asked gently, his eyes shaded by his hat, his mouth held tautly.

She held it out. "You can read it if you wish. It said it wasn't suitable to their list. That I need more practice before coming up to their standards."

He scanned the single sheet, then handed it back. "Maybe you could try another publishing house."

She nodded. That would give her something to do when she reached her father's. She tried a smile. "I'll be all right. It was just the disappointment on top of everything else." Oops. Shifting uneasily, she looked beyond Kyle to his horse. The animal stood relaxed in the hot sun, one hind leg resting on his toe as he patiently awaited his rider. Ground hitched, he wasn't going anywhere until Kyle remounted.

She fidgeted beneath his direct gaze.

"I came for the mail," Maggie said, wondering how long Kyle planned to cup her face, how long she could resist throwing herself into his arms and begging for another kiss. Just one more before she left.

"That's all that came today, your manuscript?" he asked, his thumbs rubbing gently across the soft skin of her cheeks.

"Um, no I think there were a couple of other pieces." She tried to think up an excuse for not picking them up.

Kyle released her and walked to the mailbox, pulling down the front and reaching inside for the letters, circulars and bills that rested inside. He withdrew the stack and glanced at each piece. Stacking them together, he walked back to Maggie and held out the mail.

She stared at it like she'd never seen mail before, and certainly didn't want to touch it.

"You can run it up to the house," he said.

She made no effort to take the stack. Her mind went blank and the only thing left to focus on was the steady pounding of her heart, the heated blood rushing through her veins.

Kyle watched her, obviously puzzled. Then he glanced beyond her to her car. "Maggie?"

"What?" She met his gaze.

"Are you going to take the mail up to the house?"

Slowly she shook her head.

He lowered his hand. "Why not?"

"I'm not going up to the house."

With a frown, he stepped around her and walked over to her car. In two seconds he saw the computer sitting in the back seat.

"Is your computer broken?" he asked evenly, still staring into the car.

"No." She looked out at the highway. If she had not stopped for one last check of mail, if she had not opened the envelope, if she had not had a fit of crying, she would be heading down that highway now and Kyle would have been long behind her. Now he was sure—

"Maggie, what's going on?"

"I'm leaving," she said. She'd die if he tossed his hat in the air and shouted hallelujah.

But there was only silence. A car appeared on the far horizon. Maggie watched as it drew near, sped past. Slowly she turned to watch it until it disappeared. Kyle had not said a word. Finally, curious, she turned around and looked at him.

He stared at her, his expression blank. Maggie took a deep breath and with a calmness that belied the roiling emotions that churned deep inside, she walked to her car. He stood by the door, he would have to move before she could get in.

"Why?" Kyle asked.

"Surely that's obvious. I can't stay, you've already asked for a replacement. I talked to Mrs. Montgomery this morning, she's found someone. I bought plenty of food yesterday, so meals won't be a problem until the new housekeeper arrives. And all your clothes are clean, and the house—"

"You've been planning this for a while," he said.

She expected more of a reaction from him. She nodded. She couldn't bear to be so near him, loving him so much, and knowing she had to leave. Couldn't he just mount up and ride away?

"Where are you going, did you get a new job?"

"Not yet. I'm going back to my father's. We mended some fences, as I told you, and I think we might be able to get along now. At least, I'm willing to give it a try for a couple of weeks." For that she would always owe Kyle. Yet she couldn't tell him why. "Anyway, I'm sure your next housekeeper will be perfect. She'll probably always have plenty of food, have the meals ready on time and never forget to dry your clothes."

"Probably won't dye them green, either," he murmured.

Heat flushed through her cheeks. "Oh, I had hoped you wouldn't notice."

He gave a halfhearted grin. "How could I not notice green underwear?"

"It was a light green."

"But definitely green."

"I'm sorry. I—"

"You were probably daydreaming and put something green in with the whites," he guessed.

She nodded. "Maybe your next housekeeper can bleach them out."

The silence stretched out. Maggie felt as if she was dying by inches. Finally she pasted a bright smile on her face and gestured toward her door.

"I've got to go, Kyle. It's a long drive to Denver and I want to get there before dark."

"Sure." He opened the door for her, watched as she settled in, put the manuscript beside her on the seat. He could see the bouquet the men had sent her propped in the passenger seat. When she was seated, he closed the door.

Rolling down the window, Maggie smiled again, her eyes unable to meet his. She thought her cheeks would crack. Why didn't he go back to his horse, back to his ranch and let her leave in peace?

Kyle swept off his hat and leaned over until he could see through the open window. "Drive safely, Maggie," he said. Then he leaned in and kissed her. A short, sweet kiss. Raising back a few inches, he studied her feature by feature, as if committing every inch of her face to memory.

"'Bye, Kyle," she said through the thickness of tears that threatened to clog her throat.

He stood up, his hand still on the frame of the window, slapping his hat against his thigh.

Maggie turned on the engine.

"Don't go."

She looked up. Had Kyle said that, or had she imagined the words?

He gazed across the range, hat still in one hand, the other gripping her car so tightly the knuckles were white.

"Did you say something?" she asked, her heart hammering behind her breasts. Surely she had imagined the words.

He looked at her, his eyes curiously bright. The seconds ticked by slowly, slowly. He took a deep breath, then spoke so softly she almost didn't hear him. "Don't go."

Maggie turned off the engine with shaky fingers. Kyle opened the door, slid his hand beneath her arm and eased her from the car to stand before him. Dropping his hat, he drew her into his arms, resting his cheek against her hair.

"Kyle?" Maggie was afraid to trust her feelings, afraid of the ray of hope that burst through her like sunshine.

"Stay with me, Maggie. Don't go."

She hadn't imagined the words. Her heart warmed, filled, spilled with love for this difficult man.

"I thought you wanted me to go."

"I thought so, too, but I don't. A few minutes ago when I realized you were seriously leaving, I felt as if a mule had kicked me. Every person I ever loved left me, Maggie. My mom and dad when they were killed. Rafe when he went on the rodeo circuit and then settled in the western part of the state. Even Angel, who would rather live in Laramie than on the ranch."

"Kyle, Rafe and Angelica didn't leave you, they have to have their own lives. You said you all get together for holidays, and Angelica and Jake were just here on a visit." Her heart ached for the loneliness in his voice.

"And Jeannie," he continued as if she hadn't spoken. "I really loved her. She was bright and pretty. But when I found her with that cowboy, something inside died. I figured if I ever married again I'd find someone like my mother."

Maggie didn't know what to say. She knew she couldn't compare to his mother. And she didn't think she could change, even for Kyle.

"I'm sure there's someone like that around. What about Gillian?"

He leaned back, tilted her chin up with a finger and brushed his lips across hers. "Gillian is an old friend from high school. If I was going to fall in love with her, I sure would have done so before now." Resting his forehead against hers, he gazed deep into her eyes. "And I don't want a mother anymore. I want a woman who enchants me so much I can hardly concentrate on work. I want a woman who delights in the simplest things, like listening to a man talk about his day. I want a woman who can't always get the meals right, but who brings laughter and kindness to a table of rough cowboys and who is also as tough as me."

Maggie's heart pounded. She could scarcely believe what she heard, but she wouldn't interrupt for the world. Kyle was talking about *her*. Did he mean it?

"Don't stop," she whispered, her hands pressing into the muscles of his shoulders as if she could pull him even closer.

He smiled, shook his head, rolling it against hers.

"I want a woman so innocent, she scares me. Yet so feminine I feel more masculine pride than a man ought. I want a woman who needs me, who—"

Maggie tightened her arms around his neck. "I love you, Kyle. I love you," she said, tears welling at the sweetness of his words, her heart melting at the love in his tone. Would he accept her words this time?

"I'm trying to tell you I love you, Maggie," he said, and kissed her, long and hard, then easing back until it was sweet and tender.

He pulled back and gazed down into her shining eyes. With a wicked grin, Kyle picked her up and twirled her around, emitting a loud cowboy yell. Maggie held on and laughed with the joy and love that coursed through her. Could she ever capture such rapture in her books?

He set her down and cocked his head. "So you'll stay?"

"I guess. Could I have a bit of clarification? Do you want me to stay—"

"I want you to marry me. We'll have a good life together, Maggie. You can write your books, raise the kids. We'll hire a housekeeper to do the daily chores."

"That's wasteful. I can manage."

He hesitated, took a deep breath and smiled at her. "Sure thing. There's always omelets."

"Oh, you." She punched him playfully on the arm, then gazed up at him with all the love she had in her shining from her eyes. "We will have such a wonderful life together." She paused as his words sank in. "Did you say kids?"

"Don't you want some?"

"How many?" she asked cautiously.

Kyle shrugged. "As many as we get, I guess. I want someone to leave the ranch to. Angel doesn't want it and Rafe and Charity seem settled on her place. I'd like a couple of boys, a couple of girls."

"Sounds good to me." Four, she could deal with four. Slowly she smiled, she could probably handle anything with Kyle by her side. Slowly he rubbed her body with his until his mouth moved over hers and Maggie rejoiced. She could deal with bossy men, as long as they loved her.

Samuel Foster cleared his throat. Maggie looked up and smiled at her father. He'd been visiting for almost a week. It had been a stormy few days, but they were closer than they had been since she was a little girl.

"You were a million miles away," he said gruffly.

"Just thinking." Smoothing the skirt of her wedding dress, she checked in the mirror one last time. The short dress flared out nicely. The picture-book hat made her seem as innocent as Kyle had said. But after today that would all change!

"Ready, honey?" her father asked. "You're sure about this?"

"Yes, Dad. I'm as sure as I've ever been and as ready as I'll ever be. I thought you liked Kyle." Maggie looked at her father in some surprise. He'd met Kyle several weeks ago, had stayed at the ranch for a long weekend before coming up earlier in the week for the wedding today.

"I do. I just want you happy."

"I'm so happy I almost float," she said, tucking her arm in his.

"I always thought you'd get married in a church," he murmured as they walked into the hall from her bedroom. Pausing at the top of the stairs, they looked down to see the crowd in the hallway, heard the voices in the living room. For a moment Maggie wondered if she should have chosen a church. The house over-flowed, not all the guests would get a unobstructed view of them exchanging their vows.

"No. This is better," she said.

"Why?"

She smiled at her father. "Anytime Kyle gets bossy or wants to pick a fight, I can walk right into the living room and remind him of when we exchanged vows in that very room! I figure it will be enough of a diversion to change his mood."

At first Maggie had wanted to have the ceremony in their office, where they had spent so many hours practicing for her books. But the room was too small, too crowded with furniture. The ceremony would have to be in the living room. Close enough.

As the music started and she and her father slowly descended the stairs, Maggie's gaze scanned the gathering. All the ranch cowboys were there, dressed up so much she almost didn't recognize them. Jack smiled warmly. Lance winked at her. Amused, she looked away quickly; had Kyle seen?

She knew Lance loved teasing Kyle, and her future husband never disappointed. One day he'd figure it out, stop reacting, and the fun would go out of it for Lance.

They reached the archway from the hall and Maggie saw Kyle. She smiled, her fingers trembling. It was real, they were getting married. He loved her as much as she loved him and today they were pledging their lives to each other.

She scarcely noticed Angelica and Jake, Rafe and Charity and their little boy, the friends she'd made recently and the ranch hands. She had eyes only for Kyle.

"Be happy, little one," her father said as he placed her hand in Kyle's stronger one.

"I will, Dad, forever." Maggie smiled and stepped up beside her love.

EPILOGUE

MAGGIE hummed happily to herself as she drove the big blue and white pickup truck down the highway. She was on her way home. As soon as she reached the ranch she would go looking for Kyle. She knew she would burst if she didn't tell him soon. The trip to the doctor's had only confirmed what she suspected. They were going to have a baby in a few more months.

She slowed by the mailbox and drew to a halt. Scanning the horizon, she didn't see a sign of any of the cowboys. They must be on another part of the range. So much for hoping Kyle would see her from the hill and ride down to greet her like he sometimes did.

The last two years had been wonderful. She occasionally forgot a meal, or to dry the clothes, but Kyle usually said he didn't mind. And if he started fussing, she dragged him into the living room, by the mantel, and kissed him until he was in a better mood. She smiled. She liked making up with her husband.

Of course she liked it when they didn't fight. He needed no excuse to sweep her up into his arms and carry her to their bed. Or shove the papers off the desk and make love to her there. Or in the barn when the cowboys—

Maggie shook her head. She was daydreaming again. She climbed out of the truck and went to get the mail. Another large brown envelope. Her heart sank. Another rejection? She ripped off the flap and withdrew the letter. Yes. This made the fourth book she tried. And this was the third rejection for this particular manuscript.

She scanned the sheet and grinned. There were many reasons for the work being returned. There always were. But like several of the previous rejections, this one complimented her on her warm and exciting love scenes.

She tucked the letter back into the envelope, gathered the rest of the mail and started the truck. Not that she had told Kyle about the rejection letters. She let him offer to help her practice some more so her writing would improve. She grinned in delight. There would be more practice tonight. She could hardly wait.

Glancing at her watch, her eyes widened. Ohmygod, it was late and she had not put a thing on for dinner. Not omelets again!

WELCOME TO *Love Inspired* ™

A brand-new series of contemporary inspirational love stories.

Join men and women as they learn valuable lessons about facing the challenges of today's world and learn valuable lessons about life, love and faith.

Look for:

The Risk of Loving
by Jane Peart

The Parson's Waiting
by Sherryl Woods

The Perfect Wedding
by Arlene James

Available in retail outlets in August 1997.

LIFT YOUR SPIRITS AND GLADDEN YOUR HEART with *Love Inspired* ™!

Take 4 bestselling love stories FREE

Plus get a FREE surprise gift!

Special Limited-time Offer

Mail to Harlequin Reader Service®

3010 Walden Avenue
P.O. Box 1867
Buffalo, N.Y. 14240-1867

YES! Please send me 4 free Harlequin Romance® novels and my free surprise gift. Then send me 6 brand-new novels every month, which I will receive months before they appear in bookstores. Bill me at the low price of $2.67 each plus 25¢ delivery and applicable sales tax if any*. That's the complete price and a savings of over 10% off the cover prices—quite a bargain! I understand that accepting the books and gift places me under no obligation ever to buy any books. I can always return a shipment and cancel at any time. Even if I never buy another book from Harlequin, the 4 free books and the surprise gift are mine to keep forever.

116 BPA A3UK

Name   (PLEASE PRINT)

Address   Apt. No.

City   State   Zip

This offer is limited to one order per household and not valid to present Harlequin Romance® subscribers. *Terms and prices are subject to change without notice. Sales tax applicable in N.Y.

UROM-696   ©1990 Harlequin Enterprises Limited

HARLEQUIN AND SILHOUETTE
ARE PLEASED TO PRESENT

Love, marriage—and the pursuit of family!

Check your retail shelves for these upcoming titles:

July 1997
Last Chance Cafe by Curtiss Ann Matlock
The most determined bachelor in Oklahoma is in trouble! A lovely widow with three daughters has moved next door—and the girls want a dad! But he wants to know if their mom needs a husband....

August 1997
Thorne's Wife by Joan Hohl
Pennsylvania. It was only to be a marriage of convenience—until they fell in love! Now, three years later, tragedy threatens to separate them forever and Valerie wants only to be in the strength of her husband's arms. For she has some very special news for the expectant father...

September 1997
Desperate Measures by Paula Detmer Riggs
New Mexico judge Amanda Wainwright's daughter has been kidnapped, and the price of her freedom is a verdict in favor of a notorious crime boss. So enters ex-FBI agent Devlin Buchanan—ruthless, unstoppable—and soon there is no risk he will not take for her.

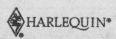 

HARLEQUIN WOMEN KNOW ROMANCE WHEN THEY SEE IT.

And they'll see it on **ROMANCE CLASSICS**, the new 24-hour TV channel devoted to romantic movies and original programs like the special **Romantically Speaking—Harlequin™ Goes Prime Time.**

Romantically Speaking—Harlequin™ Goes Prime Time introduces you to many of your favorite romance authors in a program developed exclusively for Harlequin® readers.

Watch for **Romantically Speaking—Harlequin™ Goes Prime Time** beginning in the summer of 1997.

If you're not receiving ROMANCE CLASSICS, call your local cable operator or satellite provider and ask for it today!

ROMANCE CLASSICS

Escape to the network of your dreams.

See Ingrid Bergman and Gregory Peck in *Spellbound* on Romance Classics.

As Seen on TV!

Free Gift Offer

With a Free Gift proof-of-purchase
from any Harlequin® book, you can receive
a beautiful cubic zirconia pendant.

This stunning marquise-shaped stone is a genuine cubic
zirconia—accented by an 18" gold tone necklace.
(Approximate retail value $19.95)

Send for yours today...
compliments of ✿HARLEQUIN®

To receive your free gift, a cubic zirconia pendant, send us one original proof-of-purchase, photocopies not accepted, from the back of any Harlequin Romance®, Harlequin Presents®, Harlequin Temptation®, Harlequin Superromance®, Harlequin Intrigue®, Harlequin American Romance®, or Harlequin Historicals® title available at your favorite retail outlet, together with the Free Gift Certificate, plus a check or money order for $1.65 U.S./$2.15 CAN. (do not send cash) to cover postage and handling, payable to Harlequin Free Gift Offer. We will send you the specified gift. Allow 6 to 8 weeks for delivery. Offer good until December 31, 1997, or while quantities last. Offer valid in the U.S. and Canada only.

Free Gift Certificate

Name: _____

Address: _____

City: _____ State/Province: _____ Zip/Postal Code: _____

Mail this certificate, one proof-of-purchase and a check or money order for postage and handling to: HARLEQUIN FREE GIFT OFFER 1997. In the U.S.: 3010 Walden Avenue, P.O. Box 9071, Buffalo NY 14269-9057. In Canada: P.O. Box 604, Fort Erie, Ontario L2Z 5X3.

FREE GIFT OFFER   084-KEZ

ONE PROOF-OF-PURCHASE
To collect your fabulous FREE GIFT, a cubic zirconia pendant, you must include this original proof-of-purchase for each gift with the properly completed Free Gift Certificate.

084-KEZR